FABLES
&
OTHER LIES

A Gothic Romantic Novel

CLAIRE

NEW YORK TIMES BESTSELLING AUTHOR

CONTRERAS

Fables & Other Lies
Claire Contreras
© 2020 Claire Contreras
Cover design By Hang Le
Edited by Erica Russikoff
Proofread by Janice Owen
Formatted by Champagne Book Design

ISBN: 978-0-9983456-8-0

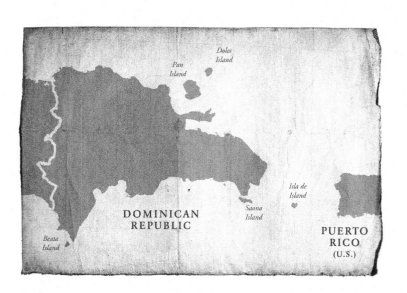

Dolos
Island

Pan
Island

Isla de
Island

Saona
Island

DOMINICAN
REPUBLIC

PUERTO
RICO
(U.S.)

Beata
Island

For Gia Guzman, my Wela.

My paternal grandmother, who helped shape who I am today, was illiterate. In lieu of reading stories to me, she'd re-tell folklore she knew. Folklore that make up the fabric of the Dominican Republic, but originated in Africa.

She seemed to have an endless library of these stories. Sometimes she'd mention them while cooking. Other times, she'd use them to heed warnings. I don't think she meant them to inspire me, but, they sure found their way into this book.

Although this isn't a folklore, per se, I included some in the story.

I absolutely loved writing this book. It very much provided the escape I needed from the reality (or alternate reality? Lol) that is 2020. I hope it does the same for you!

XO,
Claire Contreras

TERMS:

Wela: grandma

Papi: Dad

Mami: Mom

Don: Mister

Doña: Mrs.

La Ciguapa: Mythical being

FABLES

&

OTHER LIES

PROLOGUE

"I FOUND HER," HE SAID LOUDLY.

Someone walked quickly into the room. I turned to see the guard who'd been standing by the door.

"Sir, I am so sorry, I didn't—"

"The search is over. I found her," River said again.

"What are you talking about?" My heart pounded in my ears.

"This woman will keep me company tonight," he said, ignoring me.

I wasn't sure who he was speaking to anymore, but then I turned and noticed the tent drapes had been pulled open and the line of women and the people standing all around outside the tent could see us. Maybe I'd drunk too much tequila, but I could have sworn he just said I'd be keeping him company tonight.

I turned to face him. "I'm sorry, my name wasn't on the list. I wasn't even—"

"You're my pick, Penelope Guzman."

"But I didn't even sign up for this."

"You didn't have to." His smile was wolfish, territorial. "I'm the host of Carnival this year and I'm choosing to spend my night with you."

"I . . . " I looked around again, at a loss for words. I was entirely too inebriated to fully grasp what was happening, so I said the first thing that came to mind: "Our families hate each other."

"Tell me something I don't know." He was no longer smiling, but he looked just as amused as he did a minute ago.

There was a glow in his eyes, a glint. He still didn't look nice, but the adrenaline coursing through me was too palpable for me to turn away, to yank my hand from his, and if I'd really been analyzing what I was feeling, I would classify it as excitement. The most powerful man on the island, the most sought after, the most mysterious, the one I was told to never, ever summon by name, was holding out his hand for me. I set my hand over his and he held it gently as he watched me. I left it there, ignoring the shiver that slithered down my spine. *Wela was going to disown me for this.* I felt that warning in the pit of my stomach and it was only then that I pulled my hand from his.

"What happened, little witch? You remembered who you were?" River chuckled.

"I'm not the witch here." I met his gaze. "And I'm not little."

"No, not at all." He looked amused. I was annoyed.

"Why'd you pick me?"

"Why wouldn't I?"

"There are a lot of women on the island."

"Why'd you stand in line?"

"I thought it was the bathroom."

"Really?" He brought a fist up to cough into it, hiding a laugh.

"I'm not joking." I clenched my shaky hands into fists.

"I didn't think you were."

I swallowed. "So, why would you pick me?"

"Why would I not?"

I blinked, shaking my head. We were getting nowhere fast. "What am I supposed to do? As your chosen companion, I mean."

"Spend the night with me."

"Oh." I was finding it difficult to breathe, let alone speak. "And if I don't?"

"You have to."

"Says who?"

"The law. You should thank your father for that one. Oh, that's right, you can't." He grinned; it was a slow, sexy grin that made my stomach flip despite myself. "You either spend it with me or spend it in jail, and you know the conditions of these jails."

"I don't like to be given ultimatums."

"If you don't like ultimatums, you shouldn't have come to Carnival. The moment you did, you sealed your fate." He closed the distance between us again. "As a matter of fact, the moment you came back to the island, you sealed your fate."

CHAPTER ONE

I CLOSED MY EYES AS I LEANED AGAINST THE DIRTY WINDOW OF THE bus. We'd been riding for an hour and only had about fifteen minutes left to go, as long as Doña Mercedes didn't raise her hand and decide she needed to stop at the rest stop.

Again.

"So, is this your first time in Pan Island?"

I kept my eyes closed even though I knew feigning sleep would be futile. I'd only met Martín one hour ago, when we boarded the bus. I guess he figured since we were about the same age, he'd sit beside me, instead of risking sitting beside a grandmother who would chat his ear off. He salvaged his own ear in spite of mine and by the way he kept staring at my breasts every time the street went from paved to gravel and bumps, I knew he had other things in mind as well. He could stare all he wanted. It wasn't going to happen. A part him must have known. He'd gotten less and less talkative as the journey went by and my eyes wouldn't quit shutting from exhaustion, which he may as well have taken as disinterest. We were almost at our final destination now and he'd only said those nine words in at least ten silent minutes. At least he smelled good.

"It's okay. You don't have to tell me." His voice was resigned, and even though I'd been hoping he'd shut up, a part of me felt bad. I knew what it felt like to speak and not be heard.

"How many times have you been to Pan Island?" I opened my eyes and looked at him.

"About five. Mostly for haunts and excavations." He nodded at my camera. "Is that why you're visiting again?"

"No." I gripped the camera a little tighter as the guilt gnawed at me.

In the last six years, Pan Island had received over 12 million tourists. Pan was tiny and cloaked in mystery, or at least it was before the tourists decided to make it their stomping grounds, and I was partially to blame for it, with my photographs and social media engagement. The bus stopped moving with a loud squeak. Even the tires were tired of carrying unwanted people through these unpaved roads.

"The ferry leaves in ten minutes," the driver called out. "I tried to make it as fast as we could, but the stops . . . " He shook his head, shooting a salty look at Doña Mercedes, who scoffed and proceeded to set him in his place.

We got off the bus and collected our belongings, walking over to the ferry and showing the attendant our pre-purchased tickets.

"So, what brings you all the way out here?" Martín walked faster to catch up to me.

"I'm from Pan."

"You're kidding." He eyed me closer, looking at me up and down. "You don't look like you're from Pan."

"If I had a dollar for every time I heard that." I rolled my eyes. "What exactly does a person from Pan look like? What does a person from anywhere look like nowadays for that matter?"

"You're right." Martín nodded slowly. "It's just, I've never met anyone who's actually from there. I mean, aside from the business patrons, and they're not exactly the most welcoming unless they want to rip you off."

"Well, I don't think they approve of people excavating." I shot him a look. "If there was gold in our caves, we would have found it by now."

"The Guzmans maybe." Martín scoffed. "They're the only ones with access to those caves."

I swallowed hard and kept my eyes on the ferry as we walked on, and then on the ground to make sure I didn't slip. My Gucci loafers were a cute token of my work ethic, but they were not boat-deck approved.

"The old man Guzman died," Martín said after a moment. "Is that what you're here for? It's crazy that his funeral will take place at the same time as Carnival."

"It is crazy." I sighed heavily. "But people die all the time. Especially on Pan Island."

"Yeah." Martín's amusement suddenly dulled. "A few friends of mine died in that boating accident two years ago."

"I'm sorry for your loss."

"They were fishing off the coast of Dolos. I told them it was a bad idea, but they did it anyway." He glanced away.

I followed his gaze to the beautiful Dominican sand and

swaying palm trees we were leaving behind. How many people had sailed away from that island to hop over to mine only to never return? Too many, and the amount who had sailed away from mine to hop to Dolos Island and came back was far greater. People didn't make it out of Dolos. Not unless they were invited and one could only get invited this week. The week of Carnival.

"Have you ever been?" Martín glanced over at me.

I shook my head. It wasn't a complete lie.

"So, you've never met a Caliban face-to-face?"

"I can't say that I have." I let out a laugh. "You talk about them like they're some mythical creatures and not just another rich family."

"No. The Guzmans are just another rich family." He shot me a pointed look that made me glance away briefly. "The Calibans are the stuff of legend."

I raised an eyebrow. "Only because of the Guzmans."

"You mean because of the curse the Guzmans set on them." He raised an eyebrow right back.

"I don't believe in curses." I rolled my eyes. "My point is, they're just people."

"People you've never met."

"People I have no intention of meeting, ever."

"Damn. You're a Guzman, aren't you?" His brown eyes searched mine for a moment. "Hey, it's nothing to be ashamed of."

"I'm not." I swallowed and looked away, back at the palms that were now nearly out of sight.

I used to take pride in my family and our name. We'd fought for freedom against slavery and became free people, we'd taken part in women's suffrage and built our own town, and yet, the Guzman name had been reduced to one thing: the war between our family and the Calibans and the supposed curse that plagued their island and the water between ours.

"I'm sorry," Martín said, "I know Maximo Guzman was a very important member of your family."

"Thanks." I blinked the tears swelling in my eyes and composed myself before looking at him again. "So, where in DR are you from?"

"How do you know I'm from DR?" He raised an eyebrow. I shot him a look that made him laugh. "The capital. Born and raised. I did study in Connecticut for high school and college though."

"Why'd you move back?"

"Home is home." He shrugged a shoulder, smiling. "Besides, I'm hoping to make a name for myself in journalism. Everyone says newspapers are dead, but I want to bring them back and show people that they're not."

"How in the world are you going to do that?"

"I don't quite know yet." He chuckled. "It's another reason I love coming to Pan Island." He said it as the ferry began to dock, perfect timing. We held on to the bars in front of us as the boat swayed slightly. "Pan Island seems to be stuck in another era, wouldn't you say?"

"That's a fair assessment." I nodded. I left six years ago and hadn't returned, but I'd kept in touch with my best friends and they were always complaining about the lack of change. "So, that's what brought you here? To study the way of ancient times? I can't imagine someone dressed like you appreciates *mosquiteros* and outhouses."

"I don't." He laughed. "But Carnival is this week. I

FABLES & OTHER LIES

figured I'd enjoy it while I'm here. Besides, I was invited to the Caliban Gala."

"Oh." My brows rose. "You're brave. You lost friends just off the coast of that island and you're still willing to visit?"

"You know the tides dry up this week between the islands. I'll be fine." He smiled. "So, have you visited since you left?"

"Nope." I gave a half-hearted smile. "I don't do haunts."

It was a total lie. My job was haunts. Or rather, taking photographs of places people believed were haunted. I was proud of what I had been able to accomplish with a camera in my hand, even if it was also what tore my family apart. When I was seventeen, my father gave me a spanking new Canon for my birthday. It was the most impressive gift he'd ever given me. More so than the Cartier watch he'd given me the previous year or the pale blue Vespa he'd purchased for me just a month shy of my birthday, a token of celebration for my early high school graduation. Little did either of us know how much trouble that Canon would bring. I'd taken photographs of our island, of the fog that never seemed to lift, even on the beaches that were visited by tourists from all over the world, not because of the sunny blue skies and palm trees, but rather their lack thereof. The photograph that really brought me success was the one I didn't remember taking at all. It was a picture of Caliban Manor, a black estate, perched high on a hill, so secluded and covered in fog that no one had ever taken a clear picture of it until I did.

That picture had been the stepping stone to my successful career taking pictures of abandoned places and old houses, but it had also caused an irreparable rift between my family and me. It had gotten me kicked out of my house at seventeen and left me to fend for myself. Thankfully, I had great friends who had good families, and landed on my feet. It didn't change the fact that I lost my father that night, lost my mother by association, and had a strained relationship with my grandmother, the person who had been closest to me.

Through the years, I'd been asked countless questions about that photograph and still couldn't quite come up with a clear answer for them. To have taken the picture, I would have had to be standing directly in front of the Manor. The only way to get to the Manor was to go to Dolos Island. There were all kinds of myths surrounding just that alone. The tide was high most of the time and the turbulent waters between the two islands meant a likely death. Historians had long deemed it unsafe. Conspiracy theorists labeled it the second Bermuda Triangle. Those of us from Pan Island saw it for what it was though. The Caliban Manor was cursed and anyone who went near it suffered greatly for it. So, the question really should have been, how did a Guzman heiress stand in front of Caliban Manor and take a picture and live to tell about it?

I wasn't sure. The only thing I knew was that the Caliban Manor had been the very first picture I posted on my website, The Haunt, and now there were Reddit message boards dedicated to deciphering everything I posted. As a side hustle to my side hustle, I took pictures for a real estate company called Old Houses Inc., which was exactly that. A real estate company dedicated to only finding and selling old houses.

"So, will you be partaking in Carnival festivities since you're here? Or go to the gala?" Martín asked, pulling me from my thoughts.

"No."

FABLES & OTHER LIES

"And definitely not going to the gala then?"

"Definitely not." I felt myself smile. He obviously didn't understand the feud between the families. Maybe he thought it was a legend, like the curse itself.

"That's too bad. It's the only time we can walk to and from the house," he said, as if that was a huge selling point.

"I know. I just don't know why anyone would risk being stuck there." I raised an eyebrow at him. "You know what they say about that house."

"I know, but aren't you curious? Don't you want to see what it's like?"

"No." It was a lie. I would give up my shiny white EF 800mm lens to walk those halls and see how it really was inside.

"You look like you would." He eyed my attire. "Dressed in all black like that."

We both reared forward, then back as the boat was parked and anchored. Martín was still waiting for my response. There were a million things I could say—I always wear all black, like Johnny Cash, like Batman—but I chose to go with the truth, one I hadn't spoken aloud to anyone at all, so why not say it to a complete stranger?

"I'm here for a funeral. Or do you suppose I should wear a celebratory color to honor my own father's death?"

CHAPTER TWO

"THE DEVIL IS LAUGHING TONIGHT, BUT HE LAUGHS ALONE," Don Jose said during his eulogy. "We will not succumb to his greed or be tarnished by his wrongdoings. Maximo Guzman was a good man, a great man. Gia Guzman is a great woman and needs our help and prayers now more than ever. May we lift her up in the light so that she will come back to us." He bowed out and walked back to his seat at the front of the church. Both women and men muttered their prayers in agreement and wiped their faces.

I stood in the back of the room, with my head bowed, thinking about how much I hated funerals. I hated the condolences that came with the side hugs, shoulder pats, and the eulogies that spoke of everyone being so perfect, when most people sitting in the room knew otherwise. We were all fallible. We were never all good, despite how much we tried to be, or all bad, despite what others said about us. I wished this entire thing wasn't so hypocritical. Maximo Guzman was a good, great man. Sure, he'd turned his back on his own daughter when she was just a kid. No one had anything to say about that? No one cared about the fact that I'd had to couch surf and pay my own way through photography school all the while my parents were sitting in their golden mansion surrounded by yes-people and praying to false prophets? It angered me to think about, so I tried to push it away, but it was no use, the anger simmered. Instead of walking toward the open casket, I walked outside, shutting my coat tightly around myself as I pushed through the cold breeze.

"Hey." My best friend Dee's voice made me glance up. She flicked her cigarette away and blew out smoke. "I've been looking for you."

"Before or during your cigarette break?"

"You know I hate funerals." She walked over and wrapped her arms around me.

"Where's Law?" I asked.

"He's around." She pulled away. "He had to leave. He and his girlfriend got into a huge argument."

"Huh. Did you get to meet her?"

"No, she was too spooked by the island to even come out for drinks last night." Dee smiled, shaking her head. "Her loss."

"Yeah. Her loss." I smiled back. "Speaking of drinks . . ."

"Yeah, let's go to Dolly's. I'm sure she'll be happy to see you and serve you until you get so drunk you won't even remember this awful time."

"I doubt anything can make me forget this." I linked my arm around hers.

"How was the ride over? I'm not going to lie, I can't believe you took that shitty bus." She smiled as we walked, the gravel beneath us crunching underneath our boots.

"It was fine. I mean, it had four wheels and brought me over. It was safer than the alternative."

"I'm sorry." She groaned. "Have you been to visit your mom yet?"

"Not yet. I'm not sure that I'm ready to see her."

The truth was, I wasn't even ready to be back here at all. My parents had been in a freak accident when their seaplane went down. By all accounts it had been a clear day, which wasn't uncommon in the summer. Those who saw the plane go down assumed it would be fine, as it was already landing and grazing the water, and then everything went wrong. The clouds turned black, the fog lifted out seemingly of the ocean, and lightning struck. An awful combination that sounded more like something from a Hollywood movie than real life, but it was, and there was enough video evidence being sent all around the world for anyone to question the story's validity. Ever since the accident my mother had been flowing in and out of consciousness, at home, with nurses watching her twenty-four-seven, and my father suffered a heart attack as he was being pulled out of the plane. None of it made any sense, but here we were.

"Do you think it was the curse?" Dee asked, a whisper, as we reached our Vespas—hers bloodshed red, mine pale blue—and picked up our helmets, securing them on our heads.

"I don't believe in the curse. You know that."

"Still, Penny. You saw the video." Her eyes widened beneath the clear plastic of the helmet. "You can't deny how crazy that was, and with everything else . . . "

"I don't believe in curses." I turned around to get on my Vespa. "I'll meet you at Dolly's."

I really didn't believe in curses, but there was no denying that something evil lurked on this island. Whether it came from the Caliban Manor or our own, or the village, I didn't know, but it was there. Not one Guzman had lived a long, happy life, free of health issues or a tragic death. As far as I knew, the Calibans suffered the same fate. When I lived here, I'd made it a point to keep them out of sight, out of mind. The less I thought about them, the fewer chances I had of welcoming any of that into my life. When I reached Dolly's Bar, I parked, switched off my motor, and took off my helmet, hanging it from the handle. I watched as Dee did the same beside me. Inside, we sat in our usual booth, one we hadn't sat in for over six years.

"It feels so strange to be back here," I said after we placed our drink orders with Dolly.

"Mind if I join you?" The familiar voice was Martín's. He was dressed in a dark blue polo shirt and khakis.

"You still stick out like a sore thumb," I said. "No one here wears khaki."

His smile fell. "Is that why I just paid thirty-five dollars for a rum and coke?"

"Uh, yeah." Dee laughed. "And you may join us, if that's okay with Penny. I'm not sure what's going on here." She signaled at Martín and me.

"Oh. No." I shook my head, frowning slightly. "We just met today. Nothing is going on."

"She was kind enough to let me talk her ear off," he said, then looked at me. "Mind if I join?"

"Not at all." I started to scoot over, but Dee beat me to it, and from the twinkle in her eye I could tell she was interested. I laughed lightly and glanced away just in time to see Dolly bringing us our drinks.

"Oh, this young man is with you?" She set a martini in front of me and a whiskey on the rocks in front of Dee. "You should have told me."

"Just so you know, we're paying regular price." I winked, getting a laugh out of her.

"I wouldn't dream of charging you any more than regular price." She winked as she started to walk away. "You haven't been here in a while, but you can order with the tablets on the table and they'll bring your food right out."

"Thanks, Doll."

"Anytime, love."

"Thirty-five dollars?" Dee whisper-shouted. "She must be making a killing this week."

"You're not kidding." I looked around the bar. "I don't think I see one familiar face. Has it been like this every year?"

"Not really," Martín said, setting his drink down. "I've been here for the last three and this is the most crowded I've seen it."

"Wow." I sipped on my martini.

"I usually leave for Carnival," Dee said, "I mean, I haven't lived here for what, four years now? But even then, when I come back home I make sure not to come this week."

"I can't imagine being from here and not reveling in this," Martín said.

"That's because you're not from here," Dee and I said at the same time, then laughed.

"Oh, come on, it can't be that bad." He shot the two of us a look. "Besides, I already told you, I enjoy haunts."

"So does Penny and you won't catch her on this island unless it's an emergency." Dee chuckled, then jutted her chin out to me as she sipped her drink. "Did you tell him about your photography blog?"

"No." I shot her a look. "I don't make it a point to tell strangers about my work."

"What photography blog?"

"The Haunt," Dee provided.

"The blog? No fucking way." Martín's jaw dropped momentarily. "You run that? I thought you didn't like haunts."

"I lied. Sue me." I rolled my eyes and focused on my drink.

"Not to be a fanboy or anything, but I'm on there every single day. Do you ever look at the message boards? I'm FableKing66."

"Nope." It was another lie. FableKing66 was one of my biggest contributors as far as theories about the haunted houses went.

"She's lying. She just hates attention," Dee said. "I bet she can tell you the last time you posted."

"Maybe a year ago, but not anymore." I laughed.

"Right, I forgot, you passed the million followers threshold." She rolled her eyes, but she was smiling.

"Do you know Goddess19?"

"Of course. She starts most of the topics."

"She's sitting right beside you." I nodded at Dee, who was now blushing furiously.

"You're kidding." Martín looked at her, mouth agape. "Dude!"

"Oh my God, Penny." Dee was still blushing and still trying to hide behind her drink. "It's like your own little fan club meetup right here on Pan Island."

I laughed loudly. Martín was still shell-shocked, apparently, because he was looking between Dee and me and not saying much, which was odd for him as far as I knew.

"Are you going to the party at Caliban Manor?" he asked Dee finally.

"Are you asking me to accompany you? Because I wouldn't be opposed."

"Sure, why not?" Martín smiled, then looked over at me. "Do you have any jobs while you're here?"

"Actually, I do." I smiled. "They sent me an address." I pulled out my phone and looked at the email from Exclusive Real Estate again. "Actually, they sent me a pin location."

"What would you need a pin for if you have an address?" Martín frowned.

"Sometimes the GPS doesn't have the location of these old houses since they're so far off the road. Pin drops work best."

"Especially here. I pin drop and I'm from here." Dee laughed. "I mean, really. I only pin drop with Ubers."

"When are you going to take the pictures?" Martín asked. "Can we come with?"

"Sure. If you don't mind leaving now." I finished off my martini and looked outside at the gloomy skies. "This is as light as it's going to get today."

Martín and Dee both finished off their drinks. We set money on the table for Dolly and walked out of the bar.

"Should we walk?" Martín asked. "I don't have a ride."

"You can ride with me," Dee said, then shook her head. "You know what? It's better we walk. I only had one drink, but last time I drove here after one drink I spent the night in jail."

"And on the paper the following morning." I raised an eyebrow at her. "My grandmother sent me a picture of the front page."

"With a warning about how your friends suck, I'm sure." Dee scoffed.

"You know it." I winked.

"I find it fascinating that Pan Island is so conservative, yet hosts the most liberal carnival every year." Martín shook his head. "I mean, last year there were people walking around naked."

"That's Pan for you." I shrugged a shoulder and looked at the red dot on my phone. "It's this way."

We started our trek uphill and I was definitely glad we'd agreed to walk instead of drive. The island was a series of hills and curves, and even though I'd only had one drink, my head was already spinning.

"What does the description say?" Martín asked. "Of the house, I mean."

"Just that it's been handed down from generation to generation, and the new owner wants to break tradition and sell." I looked up at him. "Basically, the classic Pan Island story."

"I've heard that." He stuck his hands in the pockets of his jacket. "I think that's why I was so surprised when you told me you were from here and had left."

I nodded. The typical Pan Island tale consisted of people getting married, living either with their parents or within walking distance of them, and inheriting their houses when they passed. It was the reason I was shocked to see an email from the real estate company here at all. The market was usually stagnant. The only house I'd known of to sell to an outsider was Doña Erica, and that was only because she lived alone her entire life and had no children. There was no one to inherit the property.

As we walked, we talked about the market and the craze around all things old and haunted. Martín filled Dee in on his life, since he'd already told me about it on the bus. He was a banker in the city who worked with top bank clients. He wouldn't name names, but told us they were the who's who of the city. Dee and I weren't impressed. It wasn't that gossip was beneath us, but we had enough of that on the island already and I was definitely planning to lay low this weekend. I was so busy listening to them discuss The Haunt that I nearly didn't realize the red dot stopped moving.

"It says we're here." I stopped walking. The three of us looked around. I could smell the ocean, though I couldn't see it with the fog. I couldn't see much at all, but I knew we were definitely nowhere near Dolly's Bar anymore.

"How far did we walk?" Martín asked.

"Two miles," Dee said, eyeing her exercise watch.

"This is so weird." I walked over to the street sign. "It says we're on Dreary Lane."

Dee froze. "We cannot be on Dreary Lane."

"Why?" Martín asked with a chuckle. "Because the Devil's Chair is here?"

"Don't even bring that up." Dee shot him a look. "Last time we came here . . . "

"What?" Martín was smiling now. "You got spooked?"

"The last time I was here I took a picture that gave me the career I have now. The beginning of The Haunt, you can say."

"Yeah, but only after you sat on the Devil's Chair and left crying," Dee said.

"What?" I laughed. "I do not remember that."

"I can't imagine how." Dee shook her head. "And then you left the island."

"I was thrown out of my house." I shot her a look. "Very different."

"Still. That chair brings bad luck." She shivered. "It gives me the creeps."

"Maybe all the folktales are true after all," Martín mused, looking at me.

"Honestly, I don't remember anything about that night." I bit my lip. "I remember packing my bag. I remember fighting with my dad. That was basically it."

"Maybe it was the underage drinking," Dee said.

"Probably." I took a deep breath. "I'm going to find the chair. I need to take a picture. You know The Haunt is going to love this."

"She's not wrong." Martín started walking.

"Fine, but if you experience anything weird I am leaving." She linked her arm with mine and we followed him.

"Hey, is the house you're supposed to take pictures of 999 Dreary Lane?" Martín glanced over his shoulder.

I stiffened. I knew that address but that couldn't be right. That was Caliban Manor. I took my phone out of my pocket and read the next email. It read: *Sorry, totally forgot to send the address along with that. 999 Dreary Lane. Price tag: $15 million.* My eyes widened. I read it aloud for my friends, who gasped.

"They're selling Caliban Manor?" Dee asked, her voice a bare whisper.

"I guess we're not the only ones tired of tradition," I muttered under my breath, looking up to the spot where the house was supposed to be. "Is the tide down? If it is, we should be able to walk over there, right?"

"Walk over there?" Martín scoffed. "It's a six-mile walk."

"How do you know it's six miles?"

"The invitation says it. A van will be waiting for all of the guests to drive them over to the house."

I kept my eyes on the direction of the house, the island that stood alone just six miles offshore. I could barely make out the black iron gates, but I knew they were there. It was always like this, covered in heavy fog. So much so, that some accounts claimed there was no house there at all. The disappearing house, they called it. There were endless threads about it not only on The Haunt, but all over Reddit. It was bullshit, of course, but also the reason my picture had been worth so much. No one had ever been able to get a clear picture of the house. As if having the same thoughts, Dee spoke up beside me.

"How are you supposed to capture a vanishing house?"

"I don't know."

"It won't be vanishing tomorrow, at least not for the rest of the week," Martín offered. "The gala is in two days. I'm telling you. You should come."

"Yeah right." I scoffed. "Good luck getting me invited to that."

"You can go as my date."

"I thought I was your date?" Dee raised an amused eyebrow. "But I'm willing to sit this one out for the sake of the website."

"We can all go," he said, looking at the two of us. "Come on. They didn't specify guests on the invite."

My stomach flipped at the thought of stepping foot in that house. I knew I wouldn't be welcome. Guzmans never were. A few of my cousins worked in the main house doing repairs and they'd never been received well. One of them, my closest cousin growing up, Esteban, disappeared around the property one night. *That night.* Even though he'd been a few years older than me, we were as thick as thieves. He loved adventures, which was what ultimately led to his demise. The police said he drowned while out fishing. Legend has it that if you drown in those waters, the Caliban Manor keeps your soul. It was a dumb myth that I tried not to think about, the way I tried not to think about most awful things. I shoved bad thoughts into a box and stashed it away. It was the only way to stay sane.

"The Devil's Chair." Martín's announcement pulled me out of my thoughts. I looked over at him. "The fog seems to have dissipated from this area. If you want to take a picture, now would be a good time."

"You know, the elders on this island tried their hardest to take this down and couldn't," I said, walking toward it.

"It didn't always look like this?" He stood, brushing dust off his pressed pants.

"No way. It was a mausoleum for the Caliban family. At least that's how the story goes," Dee said. "The workers had enough of the wealthy and decided to riot and take down anything that resembled wealth. Of course, it's difficult to tear down limestone, so this stayed."

"Why is it called the Devil's Chair?"

"It looks like a throne," I said simply.

What was left of the mausoleum resembled a throne made of limestone. Whether the name came from the fact that people called the Calibans devils because they had so much wealth or something more sinister really was under these streets was just another thing that brought curious tourists here. I took a few pictures before placing the cap back on the lens.

"Okay, I'm done." I examined the pictures to make sure they were clear, then let the camera drop, the strap tugging as the weight of it hit the back of my neck.

"You're not going to sit in it?" Martín grinned. "You never post pictures of yourself on the site. I bet it'll get more views than anything else if you do, and sitting on the Devil's Chair, to boot." He signaled for me to hand him the camera. I took the strap off and gave it to him as I walked over to the rocks.

"You don't have to," Dee said, in the same voice she'd used that time I was dared to go inside one of our friend's dark basement.

"It's just a pile of rocks, Dee. I'll be fine." I sat down, Martín snapped some photographs, and I stood up, brushing off my pants. It wasn't dirt, it was sand, I realized. I turned around and looked at the seat again, and then the rest of the rocks. "The entire thing is covered in sand. Did you notice?"

"That's what it is?" Martín walked over, handing me back my camera before swiping his fingers over the bench and bringing it up. "Huh. That's so interesting. I mean, the beach is just steps away, right?"

"Yeah, but it's not like the water reaches all the way out here," Dee said.

"How would anyone know?" Martín looked at the two of us. "Everyone I've spoken to only tells me to stay far away from this area at night."

The three of us turned our attention to our left, where the water was supposed to be. Normally, you could hear the waves at a distance, but not tonight. Everything was quiet and none of it was soothing.

"I guess you'll have to come back tomorrow for the pictures of the house," Martín said.

"Yep. I can't see anything."

"I can see the gates now," Dee said. I looked closer. I couldn't see anything.

"The weather report says it will be clear the next two days," Martín said as we turned and headed in the direction we came from.

We were almost to Dolly's Bar when everything went dark, all of the street lights going out with a ting at the exact same time. Dee groaned.

"Did the lights just go out on the entire island?" Martín asked.

"Yep. That's what happens when you're over capacity with people," Dee said.

"Are you all right, can you guys see?" he asked.

"No." I stopped walking completely.

Between the sudden darkness and the heavy fog, I couldn't see a thing. My skin prickled. I felt as if someone was watching me, lurking in the shadows, underneath the fog. I turned around, but it was too dark to make out anything. Somehow, I just knew someone was there.

"Hello?" I called out. "Guys?"

"Where are you?" Dee asked, but she sounded farther away than she was a second ago.

I walked forward, determined to get to Dolly's. Everyone would surely be outside huddled together. The wind picked up slightly, making a low howl as it swept my hair around my face. When it stopped, I blinked and realized I was right back where I started. I could see the Devil's Chair from here, the black iron gates that kept people from going into the water and over to Caliban Manor. I shivered, turning around fully. Again, I felt as if I was being watched.

"Hello?" I called out again. "Who's there?"

"I've been waiting for you." The male voice was deep and soothing.

"Where are you?" My heart slammed as I blinked, looking around. "Who are you?"

"You know who I am."

"I don't."

"You're scared." I could hear the amusement in his voice. It made my heart beat a little quicker.

"Who are you? What do you want?"

"I thought good witches didn't feel fear. I thought good witches walked in the light, where there was nothing to fear."

"I'm not a witch."

"Hm. You sure about that, little witch?"

"I am *not* a witch." My eyes narrowed slightly. I tried to find him, but couldn't. I tried to speak again, but found that I couldn't do that either. When I finally found my voice, I screamed, "Leave me alone."

As if on my command, the street lights turned on all at once. I looked around rapidly, but there was no one there. No trace of a man, of anyone. Just as fast as he appeared, he was gone, and I was left facing the street that led down to Dolly's. I started running, heart pounding, hands sweating. When I got there, I spotted Dee and ran right up to her and Martín.

"Where were you?" she asked. "Are you okay?"

I shook my head. "No. Yes. I don't know. I need to go."

"Do you want to get a drink?" Martín asked.

I shook my head again. "I'm tired. I think everything just hit me all at once. I need to get home."

"Okay." Dee's frown deepened. "Text me when you get there."

"I will." I gave them each a kiss on the cheek and turned around, but stopped walking as something up the hill caught my eye.

"Huh." That was Dee, behind me. "I don't think I've ever seen a light on at the Caliban Manor that clearly from down here."

"That is odd," Martín said.

"It is odd," I said, shivering uncontrollably. "I'll see you guys tomorrow."

As I walked away and headed home, I couldn't stop thinking about it. What had happened to me? Who had I seen? I couldn't be sure, but I had too many things on my plate to worry about right now. Still, I couldn't deny that something about that light, that hill, that chair, seemed to call me and I needed to find out why.

CHAPTER THREE

Evidence of my father's chain-smoking lingered throughout the house long after he was gone. I couldn't take a breath without thinking of him. Smoking was a terrible thing, of course. For the lungs, for others' lungs, but even though I later developed an allergy to it, I never minded when Papi did it. It was part of him, like I was. As I sat on the couch, it was the scent of the cigarette smoke stuck to the couch that made me break down in tears, because it finally hit me that I'd never see him again. I'd never get a chance to redeem myself in his eyes. That last bit was what hurt the most. I'd worked hard because I needed money to live, but mostly I just wanted to make my father proud, and for what? He'd never called.

I heard voices coming from my mother's room; the nurse who was watching over her was watching a telenovela.

my face in my hands. At least I still had her to make amends with, though I wasn't sure I would. I knew myself. I knew her. We were both stubborn as goats. My father was like that as well, but my mother was worse about things. Judgmental. One-sided. After sitting there for a little while, looking at the television in front of me but not really paying attention to what was actually playing, I pulled my computer onto my lap and uploaded the pictures of the Devil's Chair I'd taken. I must have fallen asleep at some point, after reading some of the Reddit message boards about it, because when I opened my eyes again it was already morning.

"Don't put your foot on my couch." That was Wela. I obeyed, turning off the television and standing up to take my half-eaten bowl of Lucky Charms to the kitchen.

"I don't understand why you couldn't wait and have a real breakfast with me today. I was going to make you *mangú y queso frito*." She shook her head. "We haven't had a meal together in ages." She walked up to me and squeezed me into a hug. "I see that you're dressed so I assume that means you need to leave."

"I do, but I'll be back by dinner and I'll definitely sit with you for that." I kissed her tight curls. "I promise."

"I'm holding you to that." She pulled away and started getting things out for the breakfast she was going to make. "Carnival kicks off tonight."

"I know."

"You're not partaking in the festivities?"

"Papi is dead and Mami is, well, like that." I signaled toward her room. "How can I celebrate anything?"

"New life, *mi amor*. That's what Carnival is, after all. The fact that your father died the week of this celebration is a good thing. His soul will be welcomed by angels and live in the light."

"We'll see." I bit my lip. I didn't much believe in angels, but it was just one thing on the long list of things my grandmother and I disagreed on and I didn't want to bring it up now. I grabbed my camera bag and looped it around my neck, deciding not to. "I'll see you tonight."

"I thought you were going to hang out with those scoundrel friends of yours." She eyed the camera. "You're going to work?"

"Yep."

"Someone is selling their house here?"

"Apparently so."

"Who?"

"We don't know everyone on the island, Wela."

"Try me." She shot me a look. "What's their last name?"

"I'm not privy to that kind of information." I smiled wide and walked away quickly. "See you later!"

"Be careful on that Vespa. There have been more accidents these last two years than ever before," she called out.

"That's because the tourists don't know how to drive here."

"Be careful with those tourists!"

"I will." I strapped on my helmet and sat on my Vespa, driving it out of the neighborhood and waving at some neighbors as I went.

I thought about my mother, who I should have gone to see this morning. What if she died before I got a chance to say goodbye? The thought made my chest squeeze. That wouldn't

happen. She'd survive. She'd survive and we'd forgive and re-
pair our damaged relationship. That was what would happen.
I rode off toward Dolos Island with that thought in mind.

Wela wasn't kidding about the tourists. There were rented
Vespas everywhere and most of the people on them didn't
seem to know how to maneuver them. I held my breath as the
light turned green and hoped to God no one crashed into me.
The streets were filled with so many people that I was forced
to stay at a whopping ten miles per hour out of fear that I
might hit someone. The celebrations clearly started early,
with people spilling out of bars, laughing, and telling their
renditions of all of the horror stories Pan Island had survived.
The bits and pieces I'd overheard at stop signs and red lights
were enough to convince me not to partake in this "celebration." Carnival was something I found to be fun when I was
a kid, since I got to paint my face and dress up. It was a local
celebration. The minute the politicians opened up the ports
and allowed for tourism, it became something else. That was
also when my parents forbade me from going because they
thought it was too dangerous. We didn't know the outsiders
or what their intentions were. I didn't get to experience it as a
teenager or adult, which was the only reason a small part of
me was curious about it.

As I neared the iron gates, I slowed even more so. The
number of tourists on this side of the island was almost un-
imaginable. It had always been an attraction, even when I was
a child, but back then there were maybe a handful of people
with cameras trying to get evidence of the supposed vanishing

house. No one could get past the iron gates though, and even if they did, they'd only walk a few steps before they hit water. The house was said to be six miles beyond the gates. One mile was covered in dark sand, the rest was the ocean, and then, finally, the Manor. I'd never seen the water nor taken a boat over. It was strange, really, I had a photograph of the house that I didn't remember taking, but that day there was no water, there was no fog. It was as if the darkness lifted in the precise moment I snapped the shot and then fell upon me all over again. I parked my Vespa and looked around as I took my helmet off and put it away. Everyone was talking about the Caliban Manor and the water that surrounded it. Some were trying to figure out how they'd make it over there, if they dared. Others were talking about global warming and what that could mean for the house. I almost felt bad for the Calibans for not having privacy.

Almost.

The high tide usually served as a barrier between the Devil's Chair and the house. Even if someone wanted to walk across it, they couldn't. They'd have to boat, like some were saying, and those who boated often were never seen again. I thought of Esteban being in that dark water and shivered. A few nights a year, like tonight and tomorrow, the tide would be so low that it was almost nonexistent. On nights like these, you'd never know there was an ocean between us and them at all. The closer I walked to the black iron gates, the clearer it became that today wouldn't be a good day for photos either. The fog was clear, but still there, and even though I knew that might add to the beauty of the shots, I wasn't sure how in the world they'd let me in and keep everyone else at bay.

I took some pictures of the gate, of the street view,

figuring I'd have to photoshop everyone out of the picture, and then looked to my left and swallowed at the sight of the Devil's Chair. There was a line of people waiting to be pictured with it. A line of idiots. As I examined the pictures on the small screen of my camera, I heard the unmistakable sound of wet sand being walked on. I turned and saw a man walking over to me. A man dressed in dark pants and a dark lightweight jacket. At first glance, my heart did a little dip. He had a chiseled jaw and a head full of hair parted to the side, like an old Hollywood film star, and then he looked at me, setting the weight of his attention on me, and I thought I might stop breathing altogether. He was beautiful, gorgeous, unreal. He stopped on the other side of the gate and brought a key to undo the lock.

"I've been waiting for you," he said, and his voice, a low, sexy growl, vibrated through me. It took me a second to realize what he'd just said.

"What'd you just say?" I took a step back, stricken.

"I've been waiting for you." He arched a brow. "You are here to take photos of the house, aren't you? The real estate company sent you?"

"Yes." I cleared my throat. "Sorry. I've been distracted since I got here." I shot him a shaky smile. "So, are you going to let me in?"

"I'm actually indisposed at the moment." He opened the gate wide enough to walk out of it and locked it behind him. "I need to meet someone in town."

"Oh." I frowned and looked in the direction of the house, or where the house was, miles down. "Can't someone else show me around?"

"I'm afraid they can't."

"So, how exactly am I supposed to do my job?"

"That is a great question." He pointed at me and turned away, walking toward town. I fumbled with my thoughts for a second before following behind him.

"Um . . . hey." I rushed over to him and stopped short when he stopped walking. "I didn't catch your name."

"River." He turned to face me. He was so much taller than me, even in my platformed boots, that I needed to tilt my head to look at his face. "River Caliban."

"Caliban?" I blinked. "You're a Caliban?"

"Last I checked." His eyes danced. "Why don't you come back after the gala? The fog will still be lifted then and the house will be in a better mood then."

"In a better mood?" I felt myself frown.

"That is correct, Miss Guzman."

"You know who I am."

"Of course, I know who you are. You think I'd just let a stranger waltz into my house and take photographs?" The way his eyes burned into mine, I knew exactly what he was insinuating and because I had no way of defending the fact that I'd taken a picture of his house and published it and profited from it, I stayed quiet and bit my tongue.

"I guess I'll come back then. The gala is tomorrow night?"

"It's in two days. Carnival festivities begin tomorrow night."

"Right. So, you want me to come back in three days?"

"Yes, that should be fine." He gave a nod. "See you soon."

"Yeah." I nodded slowly, watching him go and watching the way every head turned in his direction as he walked. I wondered if they knew who he was or if they were just looking at him because he was impossible not to look at.

Closing my camera lens and putting it away in my bag, I turned around and started walking back to my Vespa. The fog was darker now, heavier. Though I could still hear tourists talking around me, I couldn't see them. Suddenly, I heard a whisper. My heart slammed against my chest. Not again. Not a repeat of last night. I walked faster.

"Penelope," the whisper said. "Penelope."

It was a familiar voice. One I hadn't heard in years and didn't want to pause for now. I picked my pace up to a jog, and then a sprint until I reached my Vespa. I didn't even get my helmet on before I started driving.

"Come back, Penelope." The whisper was louder now, growled, angry.

I slammed on the brakes. My body shifted forward as the back of the Vespa lifted in the air from the force of it. I looked back. The fog was lowering, snaking onto the street, covering the cobbled street that was just visible to me a few seconds ago. I gripped the handlebars tighter and turned the Vespa around, shining the light in the direction the voice had come from, my heart speeding up as I waited for any sign of Esteban. He was dead. I knew there was no way he'd step out of the fog. There was no way. And yet, I heard his voice as clear as day, calling out my name.

Shouts behind me got louder and I glanced over my shoulder to see the festivities were now spilling onto Dreary Lane; people had cameras pointed in the direction of the Caliban Manor. The crowd rushed toward the gates, swarming around my Vespa as if this was the Pamplona Festival and not the Pan Island Carnival. I had one foot on the ground and the other on the footrest to maintain balance as the cobblestones beneath me shook. More and more people charged toward the gates as if they were on a witch hunt, but they were all smiling, laughing, dancing around in costume, and seemed to stop as soon as they reached it. I squeezed my eyes shut as the chaos continued.

"Penny." I heard Esteban's voice again.

I opened my eyes, half expecting to find him standing in front of me. He wasn't. Still, my gaze remained fixed on the crowd in front of me, the ones in line waiting to take a picture on the Devil's Chair. It was as if something was keeping me there, watching, waiting.

"Leave me alone!" It was my shout, I realized, and I said it again, "Leave me alone."

And just like that, I was able to move again.

CHAPTER FOUR

"Wela, how did Carnival start?" I asked over a bowl of white rice and red beans.

"How did it start . . . God, it was so long ago I barely remember the story. It was the year we claimed our freedom from Spain. I guess that was it. A celebration." Her eyebrows pulled in as she glanced outside. "You know, I used to hate all of this tourism, but I kind of like it now."

I followed what she was looking at. There was a group of tourists following a guide. Some took pictures, while others simply admired the house we were in. I wondered how far the history lesson would go. Would they tell them how the Calibans tried to take over the island? And how my great-great-grandfather fought back? How they all did?

"I know the neighbors find it invasive," Wela said after a silent moment, "but it's nice to know that these houses will live on in more than just their memories."

"Do you remember that night," I started, "when Papi told me to pack my things and leave?"

"Of course." Wela met my gaze. "It was awful. Do you remember that night?"

"Bits and pieces. You said something to me, about the Calibans being responsible for what happened."

"Of course, they were." Her eyes narrowed as she shook her head. "They're devil worshippers."

"How do you know they are?"

"Because I know the history of this island." She raised an eyebrow.

"I just . . . I feel like the devil-worshipping stuff and the Devil's Chair and the disappearing house . . . they're just stories."

"Of course, you'd suggest that." She shook her head. "You think the Bible itself is a series of stories composed by men who wanted to ensure we would all be controlled."

"I don't want to discuss the Bible or argue over our religious beliefs, Wela."

I regretted the day I even brought up the topic of religion in this household. It wasn't like I didn't know any better. She was a devout Catholic, who went to Mass on Sundays, prayed the rosary, and got on her knees whenever anyone she knew was ill. She'd even managed to get some holy water from Rome, blessed by the Pope himself, and sent me away with it when I left this house all those years ago. Wela was not the one to bring questions about faith to. Not unless you wanted her to call the priest she had on speed dial so he could perform an emergency prayer over your forehead just in case.

"Why are you bringing up the Calibans now?" She sucked her teeth and glanced over at me again.

"I was just wondering why you said what you said." I shrugged. "That's all."

"Those people. That house . . ." Wela shook her head with a sigh. "It's a darn shame that they live there at all. It's the only place we can get what would cure your mother." She looked in the direction of the bedrooms.

"What do you mean? What cure?"

"There's a tree on the property that blooms every year during Carnival." She shot me a pointed look. "You asked why we celebrate. This is why. That tree is said to have magic powers. Some call it magic. We call it faith. It is said to have been brought here from Jerusalem. Planted right there, when the ocean hadn't yet become angry with its surroundings, with its inhabitants."

"So, the tree only has leaves now?" I leaned forward.

"It only blooms once a year, for one week."

"Have you ever seen it?"

"Seeing it would mean crossing the iron gates." She shook her head. "My mother saw it when my father worked there. It cured her of her suffering. The few leaves I had were used to help those in need and the rest dried up."

"Why hasn't everyone tried to cross those gates for it?"

"Who says they haven't?" She pursed her lips. "Look at what happened to Esteban."

"Hm." I nodded in agreement, then frowned. "But Tia Julia is alive."

"You know what they say about the island. It takes a life and gives another life."

I sat back in my seat. "Does she believe that?"

"Of course, she does. Why do you think she's become a hermit? She used to go out, always wore the latest fashion, painted her lips red, and then . . . nothing."

"Well, her son died. I can't imagine her going back to regular life after something like that happened."

"It was more than that. It's the Calibans." She turned to the window again. "Those leaves, like I said, they're healing leaves. In your mother's case, I'd give it to her in a tea. My mother used to make potions out of the leaves and sell it to people who wanted to forget things."

"Forget what?"

"Burdens from their trauma. It's not our place to ask those questions."

Our place meaning hers and the long line of women who came before her. Outsiders called them healers; the locals called them witches. It didn't come with the negative context that word often carried. My grandmother had helped many people. Her mother helped even more, but that was before we had doctors and nurses and hospitals. Even so, a lot of people still visited our house to seek treatment when they were out of options. It was something Wela passed down to my mother and that was where it stopped. Maybe if I hadn't been kicked out of the house and left the island I'd have followed the same lineage of work. Maybe if I hadn't found luck and a way to make a living in my own way. Maybe, but probably not, because unlike my mother and hers and hers, I questioned everything.

"So what does Papi's death mean?" I asked after a moment. "It makes no sense. Mami is really ill. Papi died. Shouldn't she be well? What does the doctor say? Have you even called him or have you been working your miracles on her instead of listening to science?"

"Of course, she's been seen by a doctor. He has found nothing. He said it's likely she's shut down because of the experience."

"So, she's not ill then, not really. How would any of those leaves help her?"

"Like I said, they heal every wound—physical, mental, everything."

"This is all so antiquated. We're not in the seventeenth century. If she's having a psychiatric break, she should be in a hospital."

My grandmother pursed her lips. "There's a nurse monitoring her day and night. You'd know that if you bothered to step foot in her room."

"That's not fair." I felt a flush of anger creeping up my neck.

"Life doesn't care about fairness. We live, we suffer, we die." She met my gaze. "You've been afforded more than most. More than all of us. You've had peace and health and happiness. You've had freedom. And yet you sit here speaking about fairness?"

I bit my tongue, unable to keep my eyes from burning. I hated when she lectured at me, but she was damn good at it, I'd give her that. We were both quiet for a moment, respectively brewing.

"As for the meaning behind your father's death," she said. "I don't know. My theory is that the island wanted you back."

"What?" I stopped breathing. "Me?"

"I think that was the reason for your father's death." She searched my eyes, as if looking for some kind of confirmation I didn't have. "I think it has unfinished business with you, and I don't know what it is, but my intuition says that you bargained with the Devil the night you sat in his chair, and now he's brought you back to collect."

"Did you see that in your tea?" I glanced at the cup beside her.

"Maybe. Not that you'd believe it if I did."

"It's kind of hard not to question that. An island isn't a person. It can't possibly need anything from me."

"An island is a piece of land like any other. All of our ancestors rest beneath our feet. Don't you think they have power?"

"If they did, why would they let my father die like that? And my mother . . . " I shook my head, standing from the table, heart pounding. "I don't believe in witchcraft and you know it."

"What I do with this tea is not witchcraft, Penelope. You know that as well as I do. I'm a Catholic, after all."

"I don't know what you people believe anymore." I began picking up the plates and taking them over to the area of the sink.

"Leave the plates."

"I'm going to set them here."

I just needed something to do. Someone would wash them. Not me or Wela, but one of the staff. Picking up my own plate and washing it was something I didn't start doing until after I left the island. I'd been so spoiled when I lived here, with my nannies and maids. It wasn't a big to-do, either. Even my maids had maids and my nannies had nannies. Normally, I'd take a moment to get to know them, but I'd decided that this trip I wasn't going to tie myself to anyone. I was here to say my goodbyes, my final goodbyes.

"Let me read your tea," she said.

"No." I stopped what I was doing and looked at her. "You know that makes me uneasy."

"Uneasiness is a reflection of the state of your spirit."

"My spirit is fine, thank you very much." I crossed my arms, leaning against the kitchen counter.

"Your spirit is tied to this island, and the island has been uneasy for some time now. Maybe that was why you had to come back. Maybe you're here to get those leaves and cure your mother. To right a wrong."

Goosebumps spread over my arms. "What if I die trying, like Esteban?"

"You won't."

"What if I succeed and someone else dies?" I licked my lips. "You said it gives a life and takes one away."

"That's a price you have to be willing to pay to save your mother."

I swallowed and looked away. When I looked at my grandmother again, she was turning a tea saucer slowly in her hand. I didn't want to know what she saw in it, so I stood up straight and started walking out of the kitchen.

"I'm going to see my mother." I walked to her room on the second floor, anticipation curling inside me with each step. I took a deep breath and opened her door, the low hum of the in-room air-conditioning unit greeting me. There was a young nurse dressed in pink scrubs who stood when she saw me.

"Ms. Guzman." She smiled. "I'll let you visit with her. I'll be right back." She walked out of the room.

My parents' room had two sitting areas and two walk-in closets. I took my time walking past those before nearing my mother's bed. I didn't know what I expected to see, but what I found wasn't it. She looked peaceful lying in the center of the king-size bed. Her dark golden skin a contrast against the white comforter. Her dark curly hair was pulled up into a high ponytail. I wondered how Wela was allowing that. My mother always wore her hair down, usually blow-dried straight, prim and proper to go with her makeup and designer dresses. My heart squeezed as I thought about her life before this and how it would be when she finally recovered. I pulled up one of the chairs to sit beside her hand and sighed, wondering if the heaviness I felt inside would ever lift.

Last time I'd seen her I was so angry that she didn't defend me. So angry that she'd let my father ridicule me and even more angry when I finally had spoken to her and she acted like all of it was my fault. That night was such a blur, but I remembered that much about it. I remembered crying as I packed my bags, crying harder when I realized my father wasn't joking, I had to leave his house, and I did, though a part of me hoped he'd call and apologize, asking me to come back. He never did. I could only assume he wasn't sorry. My mother, on the other hand, did call. She never asked me to come home, but she hinted that I should visit. I wish I had, but hindsight was twenty-twenty. Mami stirred in bed. I leaned forward as her eyes opened slowly, adjusting to the room, to my face.

"Penelope?"

"Mami." I reached for her hand, the grief of everything, the loss of my dad, of my relationship with him, with her, finally crashing down on me. I couldn't stop the tears that came. "I'm sorry."

"Penny," she said.

"Yes, Mami. I'm here." I squeezed her hand.

"You shouldn't be here." She shook her head. Her voice was already hoarse, but she repeated it again, this time a rough whisper, "You shouldn't be here."

"I . . . had to come see you." I swallowed, using my other hand to wipe away my tears. Wela said she hadn't told my mom about my father's death to not slow her down from recovery.

"You shouldn't be here."

"It's okay," I said. "It's okay now."

"You need to leave the island."

I sighed heavily. She really wasn't lucid and it broke my heart.

"They'll take you, Penny. Don't let them take you," she whispered, tears trickling down her face.

"I think she needs to rest, Miss Penny." That was the nurse, back from her short break.

"Has she been like this?" I let go of my mother's hand and stood as the nurse walked over and touched the IV bag, injecting a needle into one of the attachments.

"She's in and out."

"P . . . Penny," Mami said, a whisper as her eyes closed. "Get out. Please get out."

"Don't mind her, Miss. She's not herself right now," the nurse said. "This is completely normal in a breakdown. She's been through a lot."

I nodded, but a painful sob settled in my chest. I hadn't seen my mother in six years and the first time I do, she's bedridden and tells me to leave. I tried to swallow past the blockage in my throat, but couldn't. I hadn't cried in so long, but this felt like too much. After idling for a moment, I left my mother's room and went to mine. I grabbed my bag and packed the few things I'd unpacked.

"I'm going to stay with Dee," I said to my grandmother.

"Why would you do that? This is your house."

"Mami said I should leave." I bit my lip, but it was futile. Tears pricked my eyes and ran down my cheeks. "The first time I see her in ages and she tells me to leave."

Wela's frown deepened. "She said that?"

"It's fine." I swallowed hard. "I mean, it's not fine, but I'll figure something out."

"She's not in her right state," Wela said, her voice low, brown eyes compassionate.

"I know." I swallowed hard. I did know that, but it didn't make it any easier.

"She's not wrong about this island. What happened to your parents wasn't an accident."

"I saw the video. It was a total accident."

"If you saw the video, you'd know that the accident didn't kill your father, Penny. He walked out of that plane. His heart gave out on him afterward."

"Because of the accident."

"They both got out of that airplane unscathed. It wasn't until they got back on the island that things started happening, and it wasn't until you got here to pay your respects to your father that your mother's health took a turn for the worse."

"So, you're saying this is my fault." I put a hand to my heart and took a step back.

"It's not your fault. It's the curse." She lowered her gaze. "This curse will be the end of us all."

"I don't believe in curses."

"You may change your tune about that if you decide to stay longer."

With those words, I picked up my bag and walked out of the house.

CHAPTER FIVE

"I MEAN, YOU CAN'T BLAME THEM FOR BEING WORRIED." DEE shot me a sympathetic look.

She was sitting in her vanity while Jose, a masterful makeup artist, worked on her look for the Carnival kickoff tonight. The theme this year was *Black Swan* and I had to assume most people would be wearing dark makeup and black tutus. Dee was wearing a short black tutu, sky-high Alexander McQueen sandals, and a lacey black bralette. She looked hot, and after Jose was done with the dark makeup, she'd look hotter. I still hadn't decided whether or not I was going to join the festivities, which meant I wasn't. I didn't have anything to wear to it even if I wanted to and it was too late to go shopping.

"Maybe she's right about the curse," Jose said, looking at me over his shoulder. "After the life I've lived, I believe in it."

"I don't." I pursed my lips. "She basically made it sound like I was responsible for all of this."

"I think she's just worried for your safety. You know how the elders can be," Dee said with a sigh when Jose pulled away to get some fake lashes. "Just . . . stay here. Come out tonight for Carnival. I promise it'll be fun and you won't regret it."

"I don't even have anything to wear."

"That's the least of it." She turned her face back to Jose as she spoke, "Jose can do your makeup and I'll get you something from Xiomara's closet. She ran off to New York anyway. It's not like she misses anything she left behind. I bet she has some old ballet outfits."

"I don't know about ballet outfits, but she has that beautiful feathered skirt and crop top," Jose said. "She never even wore it."

"The one that gives *The Crow* and *Cruel Intentions* vibes?"

"That one!" Jose stood up. "She left it behind. I'll go grab it for you, Pen. Don't worry, we'll have you looking like the hostess of the show."

"I thought they didn't pick women to be the host." I smiled.

"They don't," Jose said as he waltzed out of the room.

"You know the patriarchy and their bullshit." Dee rolled her eyes.

I shrugged. It wasn't anything new, and it wasn't like we were the only ones stuck on that bullshit.

"I knew I'd seen it there." Jose walked back into the room with an item of clothing on either hand. "Skirt and bustier."

"That's a bra." I blinked. "My grandmother would wring my neck if she saw me out in that."

"She's not going to be there," Dee said with a laugh.

"You act like she won't know every single thing that went on and what everyone was wearing before breakfast tomorrow." I looked at the clothes as Jose walked over and touched the black feathers that looked like they were wet. The material felt glossy, almost like a dominatrix leather. I envisioned it on me—I could wear tiny boy shorts under the skirt. The feathers would hit me well above the knees. The bustier would lift my small breasts. I could wear a chunky gold necklace and a gold bracelet.

"Look at you. You're salivating." Jose chuckled then looked over at Dee. "She's totally going to wear it."

"I'm totally going to wear it." There was no use in denying it. "I am going to need you to do my makeup though."

"Girl. I'm going to do your makeup and we need to do something about that hair. That messy bun is sexy, but not for Carnival."

"Do whatever you want with me." I opened up my arms. "I'm willing to be your pet project."

And pet project I was. Between Jose and Dee, they had me ready at the speed of light. When they were finished, I zipped up my knee-high combat boots and walked over to the mirror. The red lipstick I was wearing contrasted with the all-black attire, making it the perfect combination. I smiled. I looked sexy. I felt sexy.

"You're both magicians."

"So they say." Jose winked. I laughed.

"Let's head out. I told Martín we'd meet him at Dolly's for shots."

"I cannot wait to see this Martín guy," Jose said. "Is he cute?"

"He's cute." I smiled. "He doesn't stop talking, but he's cute."

"Oh, a chatterbox with Dee?" Jose's eyes widened. "Who talks more?"

"I'm going to pretend you are not talking about me like that in front of me." Dee shook her head, smiling as we walked out of her room. "But for the record, I talk more because I have a lot more interesting shit to say."

"Right," Jose and I both said with a laugh.

"Who's the host this year?" I asked. "Of Carnival I mean."

"Oh, you haven't heard?" Jose's brows rose.

"Shit. I didn't tell you?" Dee's eyes widened as she grabbed my arm. "This doesn't change anything. We're still going."

"Don't tell me it's a Caliban." I rolled my eyes.

"It is." Dee bit her lip. "But who cares? It's not like he's going to pick you. You don't even know each other."

"Isn't Mr. Caliban old, like really old?"

"And bedridden," Jose said. "He's not the host. God. He was such a horror when he was the host. I'm kind of shocked they picked someone from that family at all."

"Seriously," I agreed.

"Who'd they pick? The son?"

"Must be." Jose shrugged. "He's become a legend around here, coming in and out of Pan Island whenever he pleases with his fancy-ass cars and model girlfriends."

"Really?" My brows rose. "Why would he come here? And how?"

"By boat, I assume."

"He takes a boat and doesn't die in those waters?" I raised an eyebrow and glanced at Dee.

"Hey, I haven't been here either. Whenever I do visit, I only hear stories about this gorgeous god of a guy. I still think it's crazy that they chose a Caliban though, hot or not."

"Same." I nodded slowly. Jose did as well.

Of course, none of us had been alive when it happened, but it was the talk of the town for years and years afterward. The curse and the Caliban Carnival was always mentioned at dinner parties even if it was just in passing, usually hushed, as if no one could bring themselves to speak the words aloud. And like everything else on this island, they called it a fable, a legend, a myth. It was the only fable I actually bought into. Some things are too horrible not to believe. Every year, the host of Carnival was the firstborn male of each household. Every night of Carnival, the man got to pick one woman to spend the night with. Single, married, widowed, it didn't matter. Most of the men on the island were respectful and responsible with this task. They picked a single crush or a woman they were already dating, engaged, or married to.

The year Wilfred Ambrose Caliban was chosen, he picked a married woman. The wife of a farmer whose beauty was said to only be rivaled by that of the sun's rays. Like most stories, there's no telling what's true and what's not. It's been passed down to so many ears and spoken by so many mouths that we can only deduce what we think may have happened, but legend has it that the woman, Sarah, was never seen again. The farmer tried, with his equipment, to take the black iron gates down himself. When he finally received word from Sarah, it was via divorce papers and an apology letter that is now framed in our town library. I read the letter many times, trying to search for clues of lies and sadness, but found none. She seemed sorry for her husband, but not sorry enough to come back. And so, with Sarah, the sun left the northern part of the island, where the Caliban residence sat. They say the farmer put a curse on it that no one, not even the most spiritual beings around here, like my grandmother and people like her, could displace because no one could erase grief like that.

"Whoa." That was Dee as we started nearing the main street of town, where everyone was in some kind of costume and walking around.

Whoa was right. The costumes were dark, but the mood was festive. Martín, who was waiting for us, spotted us quickly. He was in all black, including a top hat with a feather sticking out of it.

"Do you know what *Black Swan* is?" I asked.

"Not really." Martín grinned as he gave both Dee and me a kiss on the cheek and shook hands and introduced himself to Jose. "The three of you look like you belong on the cover of a gothic album."

"Funny," Jose said, in a tone that was anything but amused. "Are we going to do shots, or are we just going to stand around?"

"I got the shots taken care of." Martín turned around and escorted us to a small four-seater table outside of Dolly's.

"Why are you here by yourself?" Jose asked after our latest shot of Cuervo. We'd taken six already, but who was counting? Certainly not my liver. I reached for the water.

"Because my girlfriend dumped me three days before we were set to come to this and I decided to come anyway." Martín smiled brightly. "Good thing too. I wouldn't have met these two. Or you, Jose."

"You definitely won the lottery by meeting me. I'm not so sure about these two." Jose chuckled when I nudged him.

"So, where's the host?" Dee asked. "Does he walk around? How does he pick someone?"

"Haven't you been to one of these?" Martín asked. "I know

Penelope hasn't recently, but she was the only weird one in that."

"Thanks," I muttered, pouring myself more water.

"Hey, no offense."

"I'm too drunk to be offended." I waved him off. "Where does the host pick someone?"

"I've only been to one Carnival and I was fighting with my boyfriend the entire friggin' time. I didn't even have fun," Dee said.

"Ugh. Lawrence." Jose rolled his eyes.

"Exactly."

I personally liked Lawrence, but I wasn't about to state that tidbit at a table full of Lawrence haters.

"So, the host is given the full list of attendees," Jose said. "And there's a competition. Sometimes it's modeling, other times it's just . . . a throne he's sitting on and women come up to him. Most of the time they know who they're picking before they get here though. No need for all the fuss. At least that's what one of the tour guides said once."

"Interesting." Martín grabbed a handful of peanuts in the middle of the table. "I'm surprised they still serve peanuts here. In the States, you rarely see that anymore."

"Yeah, well. It's probably a good thing." Dee grabbed a handful of peanuts as well. "I only like these when I drink."

"It's the salt," I said loudly. The music was starting and the speakers sounded like they were right behind me and not a few feet away. "Also, I need to pee."

"Already?" Dee whined.

"Dude, you're going to break the seal if you pee now," Martín warned. "You'll be going all night."

"I'm well aware, but I still need to pee." I shrugged. "I have a small bladder."

"You have a huge liver is more like it," Jose said. "You took one extra shot."

"I drank like an entire pitcher of water." I stood up and grabbed on to the table as my surroundings began to sway.

"Holy shit." My friends did the same thing. We all laughed.

"Let's check out the tents. I bet the bathrooms are set up there anyway," Dee said.

"Let's."

We all walked over, me linking arms with Jose, and Martín and Dee holding on to each other. We were definitely half past drunk, which was nice. I felt . . . happy. I felt . . . free. Those were very different feelings than anything I'd felt on the island before. When I lived here, I felt trapped underneath my family's thumb. My parents were strict, but it was our last name that brought on the feeling of suffocation. Maybe it was the costume or the fact that I knew that even if the townspeople knew who I was, they'd never run to my grandmother and tell her what I was doing. She had too much on her plate to worry about yet another thing.

"I can't believe I've never been to one of these since I was a kid," I shouted.

"I heard Bad Bunny is going to be here later," Martín shouted back, looking at me over his shoulder.

"On Pan Island?" Jose and I asked at the same time.

"It's not surprising." Dee shrugged. "The Calibans have deep pockets."

"Yeah, but Bad Bunny deep?" Jose's brows rose.

"It's a short ride from Puerto Rico to Pan," Martín said. The three of us nodded in agreement.

"Fortune-teller." Martín pointed at a tent. "Let's go see her."

FABLES & OTHER LIES

"No, thanks. I have enough fortune-tellers in my life," I said. "I'm going to look for a restroom. You guys go ahead."

"Keep your phone on you," Dee said.

"I'm going to go see the tarot reader," Jose said. "She's so good."

"Better than the fortune-teller?" Martín asked, their voices drowned out as the three of them walked in one direction while I kept walking forward.

I spotted a long line of women and nearly threw my hands up in rejoice. I didn't love standing in line, but I didn't want to walk around the entire place looking for a bathroom. Besides, I had something to do to pass the time.

CHAPTER SIX

I TOOK MY PHONE OUT WHILE I STOOD THERE TO PASS THE TIME. I'D posted the pictures of the Devil's Chair on my blog and had already gotten three million hits on it. With those follows, came comments and questions. Some questions were photography questions I was always willing to answer. Others were about whether or not the houses were haunted. Those were the ones that started entertaining threads.

At the sound of a woman shouting, I lowered my phone and glanced up on high alert. It was too early for this kind of bullshit. She was walking out of the bathroom tent, wiping her face. I looked around to see who she was arguing with, but there was no one following her. *So weird.* I went back to my phone.

"That fortune-teller was dumb," Dee said, standing beside me.

"You finished that fast?"

"Girl, you've been in line forever."

"Where are Martín and Jose?" I looked around.

"Getting more drinks."

My eyes widened. I wasn't sure I could handle more drinks right now. "So, what did the fortune-teller say?"

Dee scoffed. "According to fake Ms. Cleo, I'm going to die soon and my best friend is going to get kidnapped by the Devil."

"Oh. Typical Tuesday on the island, then?"

"I guess." She let out a laugh.

"Hey, these people don't know what they're talking about." I bumped her with my shoulder.

"Don't they? Our ancestors built this island on that kind of intuition."

"On fables. You can't take these things to heart." I shot her a pointed look. "My grandmother reads tea saucers every day. If I were to believe a word she said about mine . . . " I shook my head.

"What does she say?"

"Nonsense." I shrugged a shoulder. "Who knows."

"You never listen to her, do you?" She sounded a little more upbeat now, so I smiled a little, but just barely because she wasn't wrong. "You know what? I'm going to go get my tea read while you go to the restroom." She started walking away, then looked over her shoulder with a frown. "You sure you'll be fine?"

"If you're asking if the Devil will be waiting for me in the bathroom, I think the answer is no," I said.

Dee laughed loudly. "Good luck."

Sighing, I turned my head to count how many were in

front of me. Three. I was finally almost there. I was scrolling through the comments on my pictures when I saw one that caught my eye.

BEWARE: *He who holds the keys to Caliban Manor is cursed for life.*

My heart skipped a beat. I hadn't even taken pictures of the house yet, but I knew it wouldn't sell with comments like that. I usually didn't pay them much attention, but something about it made me click on it and read the responses beneath it.

Car3092: Did you hear they're putting the house up for sale? My uncle has stories of that place, my dude. He went there in 1990 and was forever changed.

FFOE: @Car3092 I'm surprised your uncle made it out

Rose30: I've lived on the island my entire life. No one even visits that side of the island unless they're 100 years old and need some weird shit for one of their weird potions.

Car3092: @FFOE—I know. He was always surprised he made it out alive

FFOE: @Rose30 the witches? Are they real?

Rose30: depends what you classify as a witch

FFOE: Are you a witch?

Rose30: If being a badass, independent, forward-thinking woman makes me a witch, then yes.

FFOE: *eye roll*

Car3092: we're not in the 1800s anymore @Rose30

FFOE: exactly. We don't persecute people for being feminists.

Rose30: Yet this entire thread is dedicated to warning people against Caliban Manor. Why? Because its inhabitants are rumored to be witches.

Car3092: Aren't they all men?

Rose30: Men have babies?

FFOE: The surviving members are men

Rose30: Surviving members? Wtf are you people on?

FFOE: There's a curse on that house. Everyone knows it. Why else would you stay on the other side of the island?

Rose30: Because my family's from La Bahia and I prefer the sun, thank you very much

I clicked the side button on my phone and put it in my bag once the woman in front of me disappeared into the tent. Curses, witches, the darkness on this side of the island. Those were all things that had driven the tourism here for so many years to begin with, but the fact that so many who had never been here knew about it was incredible. I wondered how many hits this place got on Google Maps.

"Next." The voice snapped me out of my thoughts. I looked at the man towering over the door and stepped forward.

"I didn't realize bathrooms needed bodyguards," I said.

"This bathroom does. When you finish, exit this way. Don't take any detours." He shot me a look.

"Where would I detour to? It's a freaking tent."

"I'm just saying, you need to check in here if you're on the list." He waved the clipboard in his hand.

I nodded and ran into the bathroom. When I finished, I washed my hands and fixed the makeup under my eyes. I definitely looked drunk. I felt drunk. I laughed at my reflection as I rolled the paper towel into a ball and tossed it in the trash can beside me. When I stepped outside, I could see the back of the man's head, which meant he wasn't looking at me. I glanced over to my right. There was a hallway. I had two options: go back outside and get on that list or find out what the list was for before going back out there and trying to get on the list. I decided on the latter because fuck bodyguards. Besides, the tequila had given me the bravado I needed.

As I walked the hall, a distinct smell hit me, lavender and something else. Something familiar I couldn't quite place. The tent opened up to a makeshift lounge, with white sofas and clear tables, that looked like something you'd see in the VIP section of a club. I wondered if this was where the artists would be. The only thing I knew for sure was that if I ran into Bad Bunny here without Dee, she'd kill me. There was no one though, or so I thought until I stopped walking in the center of the room, and saw the stage ahead. There was a man dressed in all black standing there.

"Um. Hi," I said. My voice sounded meek. I hoped it didn't sound that way aloud.

"Hi." His voice was a soft, low rumble that vibrated into me and through me.

He stepped off the stage and started walking toward me. My heart thumped louder with each beat of each step. As he drew near, I was able to get a better look at him and gasped. It was *him*. Undeniably handsome with square shoulders, a defined jawline, and when he smiled, a slightly crooked tilt of his lips, which spoke of an effortless charm. By the time he closed the distance between us, I was sure I'd stopped breathing altogether.

"I've been waiting for you," he said, taking the remaining air in my lungs.

"Why do you keep saying that?"

"Because it's true."

"What do you mean you've been waiting for me? What does that mean?"

"I found her," he said loudly.

Someone walked quickly into the room. I turned to see the guard who'd been standing by the door.

"Sir, I am so sorry, I didn't—"

"The search is over. I found her," River said again.

"What are you talking about?" My heart pounded in my ears.

"This woman will keep me company tonight," he said, ignoring me.

I wasn't sure who he was speaking to anymore, but then I turned and noticed the tent drapes had been pulled open and the line of women and the people standing all around outside the tent could see us. Maybe I'd drunk too much tequila, but I could have sworn he just said I'd be keeping him company tonight.

I turned to face him. "I'm sorry, my name wasn't on the list. I wasn't even—"

"You're my pick, Penelope Guzman."

"But I didn't even sign up for this."

"You didn't have to." His smile was wolfish, territorial. "I'm the host of Carnival this year and I'm choosing to spend my night with you." He took my hand in his.

"I . . . " I looked around again, at a loss for words. I was entirely too inebriated to fully grasp what was happening, so I said the first thing that came to mind: "Our families hate each other."

"Tell me something I don't know." He was no longer smiling, but he looked just as amused as he did a minute ago.

There was a glow in his eyes, a glint. He still didn't look nice, but the adrenaline coursing through me was too palpable for me to turn away, to yank my hand from his, and if I'd really been analyzing what I was feeling, I would classify it as excitement. The most powerful man on the island, the most sought after, the most mysterious, the one I was told to never, ever summon by name, was holding my hand. I left it there, ignoring the shiver that slithered down my spine. *Wela was going to disown me for this.* I felt that warning in the pit of my stomach and it was only then that I pulled my hand from his.

"What happened, little witch? You remembered who you were?" River chuckled.

"I'm not the witch here." I met his gaze. "And I'm not little."

"No, not at all." He looked amused. I was annoyed.

"Why'd you pick me?"

"Why wouldn't I?"

"There are a lot of women on the island."

"Why'd you stand in line?"

"I thought it was the bathroom."

"Really?" He brought a fist up to cough into it, hiding a laugh.

"I'm not joking." I clenched my shaky hands into fists.

"I didn't think you were."

I swallowed. "So, why would you pick me?"

"Why would I not?"

I blinked, shaking my head. We were getting nowhere fast. "What am I supposed to do? As your chosen companion, I mean."

"Spend the night with me."

"Oh." I was finding it difficult to breathe, let alone speak. "And if I don't?"

"You have to."

"Says who?"

"The law. You should thank your father for that one. Oh, that's right, you can't." He grinned; it was a slow, sexy grin that made my stomach flip despite myself. "You either spend it with me or spend it in jail, and you know the conditions of these jails."

"I don't like to be given ultimatums."

"If you don't like ultimatums, you shouldn't have come to Carnival. The moment you did, you sealed your fate." He closed the distance between us again. "As a matter of fact, the moment you came back to the island, you sealed your fate."

Before I could question him any further, people began piling into the tent, mostly women, most glaring at me. I couldn't tell if they were upset he hadn't picked them or upset that he was the host. It was more attention than I wanted, and when the local news reporter stepped inside waving a microphone and shoving a camera in our faces, I felt my flight response kick in and barged through the ocean of people, stomping out of the tent. I didn't know where I was headed, but I knew I needed to get out of there. Back to Dolly's, I guessed, would be a good place to run. Back to my friends. Another shot of tequila sounded nice, especially now that my previous buzz had been stripped away by all of the hoopla.

CHAPTER SEVEN

"RUN THAT BY ME AGAIN," JOSE SAID. "RIVER CALIBAN PICKED you?"

"He did but it doesn't matter. I'd rather spend a night in jail than with him."

"Spend the night in jail and risk your grandmother finding out?" Dee raised an eyebrow.

"Why would she find out?" Martín set down his beer and looked at her.

"Anyone who goes to jail gets published on the front page of the paper," she said. "It's the ultimate no-no. The last thing anyone wants is for their parents or grandparents to see the paper and have their last names tarnished like that."

"Especially if you're Pan Island royalty and your last name is Guzman," Jose added.

"My last name was tarnished the day I published the

picture of Caliban Manor." I glanced away from my friends just as the front door of the bar opened and River Caliban stepped inside.

A jolt zapped through me the instant our eyes met. I'd heard about the electric pull between two people. I'd imagined it happening to me every time I read one of my grandmother's historical romance novels. I never in my wildest dreams thought it was real, but most of all I hated that it was River Caliban, of all people, who made me feel it. My entire life I'd been warned against them, and here I was, *feeling things*. Wela did always say the Devil was a charmer and if that was the case, this one had him one-upped for sure. He walked over to our table and stood beside me as if he belonged there. I swallowed, looking at Dee, across from me. Her eyes looked as wide as they'd ever been. So, did Jose's. Martín looked absolutely stunned as well, but it was he who broke the ice and extended his hand to River with the clearing of his throat.

"Martín Echevarria." He shook his hand. "I was invited to your party tomorrow night and I'm not sure how involved you were with the invitations, but I figure I should thank you anyway."

"You're welcome." River's mouth turned up. "So, I expect you'll be there with your plus one? Barbara, was it?"

"Not Barbara." Martín chuckled. "It's a long story. I will take Denise Grillon with me." He put an arm around Dee.

"Good. That's nice. It's a pleasure to meet you, Denise." River shook her hand, then turned to Jose. "You as well."

"Jose." Jose cleared his throat. "Jose Beauchamp."

"Jose Beauchamp." River gave a nod. "Will you also be in attendance?"

"The invitation must have missed my house." Jose laughed. "Don't worry, I'm perfectly fine skipping it."

"Nonsense." River frowned, then glanced over his shoulder. I followed his gaze and saw a small group of people gathered at the table beside us. Two women and one man. All dressed in black. "Miss Fabiola. Please take note of the name Jose Beauchamp. He will be in attendance tomorrow evening as well."

"Sure thing." Miss Fabiola, a pretty Black woman, maybe in her mid-thirties, said with a nod and a stiff smile. She only shot me a quick glance before turning back to her group of people. It felt like a warning.

"Now, onto other matters at hand." River brought a hand up and used his pointer to caress over my shoulder.

"I didn't give you permission to touch me." I shivered and pulled away, shooting a glare at him.

River's eyes darkened. There was no distinction between his iris and his pupil. His gaze was so intense, so alluring, that I found that I couldn't look away, even though I wanted to.

"Why did you choose Penny?" Jose asked after a moment.

"Why not?" River kept his attention on me.

"How do you even know who I am?" I asked.

"Doesn't everyone on this island know who you are? The rebellious Penelope Guzman, who took a picture of her enemies' house and made millions from it." River's tone was light, but his expression was far from it.

"Is that why you chose me? Because you want to take revenge on the person who capitalized off your family name?" I raised an eyebrow as I reached for my Lemon Drop. "I should tell you that I didn't make millions."

"Maybe not." He cocked his head. "But you made a career from it and I have to assume you're doing very well for yourself."

"I'm doing fine."

"You're doing better than fine." River chuckled, a dark, deep sound that pulled at my strings. "Mrs. Dolly is doing fine, making just enough to pay her rent every month. You're doing well enough to afford your luxurious taste in designer clothing." He raised an eyebrow. "I would assume your father cut you off the moment you left."

"Don't talk about my father." I took a healthy gulp of the Lemon Drop and glanced away.

This was one of the issues with having too many people following you on the internet. Even though most of the time I only posted photos of old houses and haunts, every once in a while when I felt cute, I posted a selfie or asked a friend to take a posed picture of myself and that was where I assumed he saw my . . . as he said, luxurious taste in designer clothing. Damn social media.

"So, what can we expect from the party tomorrow night?" Martín asked.

I was glad he took the attention off me for a moment. I grabbed my crossbody from the table. "I need to use the restroom."

I didn't wait for anyone to acknowledge that before walking straight to the back of the bar. My heart was pounding so loudly in my head I could barely think straight and I couldn't be sure if it was the amount of alcohol in my system or the fact that River Caliban, hot as he may be, had stalked the shit out of me and I was unnerved by it. He didn't even bother to deny it either. The bathroom door closed and opened right away behind me and I turned around holding my breath, half expecting him to have followed. It was Dee though.

"Hey." She walked over. "So that was weird."

"Understatement of the century."

"I mean, at least he's really hot?" She cringed even as she said it.

"He thinks he knows my entire freaking wardrobe." I paced the bathroom. "I just feel like the only reason he picked me was to show me he has a one-up on me. And to humiliate me. And gloat. And . . . take revenge on behalf of his family."

"Seriously?" Dee let out a laugh. "This isn't a movie set in the middle ages, P. If you don't want to go with him, go to jail. Fuck it. If I were you, I'd go though. I mean, he's hot, he's rich, he lives in that mansion we never really get to see. Why not take advantage and get all the pictures you can get?"

I pursed my lips, nodding. And I could get the leaves from the supposed magical tree. If there was a tree at all. It was the absolute least I could do for my family, right?

"You know what?" I nodded a little more enthusiastically now. "I'm going to do it."

"Good." Dee smiled. "And if you want to leave or feel threatened, you call the cops and then us and we'll be right over." She hugged me quickly. "Now let's get back to the table."

"Go ahead. I actually do need to use the bathroom." I smiled as she walked out.

When I finished washing my hands and left the bathroom, I felt like a woman on a mission. That was, until I ran straight into River, who was standing between the men's and women's, smoking a cigarette.

"You're not supposed to smoke indoors, you know?" I pulled back and sneezed. "Also, I should warn you, I'm allergic."

"To cigarette smoke?" He raised an eyebrow. I nodded and sneezed again. He turned and pressed the cigarette to the ashtray on the table beside him, blowing the smoke in the other direction.

"Thank you." I cleared my throat. I hadn't expected him to do that at all.

"See? I can be civil."

"I'm not sure I'd classify that as civil, but sure." I shrugged. "I have a question. About tonight I mean."

"Okay."

"I'm assuming we'll be going back to your house, but how are we getting there? The tide should be low, but not low enough to walk across." I frowned, realizing I didn't really know. "Or is it?"

"It is," he said. "I have a car waiting outside to take us back when you're ready."

"Aren't you supposed to stay for the festivities? I heard there are huge artists coming."

"I didn't come for the festivities." His smile was slow and purposeful, like a wolf ready to pounce on prey.

"You came here for me," I said.

"Beauty and brains. We have a winner." He smiled wider, and with that, escorted me outside the building through the back door.

CHAPTER EIGHT

THE CHAUFFEUR WAS THE BODYGUARD FROM BEFORE. THIS TIME, he solely focused on the road as River and I sat in the backseat of the black Rolls Royce. Truly, a luxury car. I stretched my legs fully and my toes still didn't touch the back of the seat in front of me. I closed my eyes and inhaled the leather. It smelled like one of my designer bags. I could live in this car and die happy. River's chuckle made me open my eyes and look at him. I expected him to be on his phone, but he was just looking out the window. I glanced over his shoulder to see what was so funny, but didn't see anything. It was pitch black out. He was probably plotting my demise and I was the idiot going willingly. When I looked out my window, the only thing I could make out beneath the swaying fog was the Devil's Chair. The car stopped there and my heart sped up. When I turned to ask why we were stopped there of all places, I caught the eyes of the driver in the rearview and my question died in my throat.

"The gate takes a moment," River explained.

I looked around again. "There are no people here."

"It is pretty desolate, isn't it?" He looked outside. "They must all be enjoying the concert."

"That doesn't seem right." I shook my head and looked outside again. Every window brought the same emptiness. "I don't understand. The people that . . . a lot of people come for the chair and for the house. Someone would be here, surely."

"Do you want to get out and find out for yourself?"

"No." I shivered and crossed my arms.

The gates opened, welcoming us in, as if my refusal to be near the chair was what it had been waiting for. When we drove past the gates, I turned to watch them shut behind us and felt my fate seal. I was going to the Caliban Manor and I was going with a Caliban. The heir to the house and the family's troubles. That was what my father always said about firstborns. It was the way he introduced me to all of his friends. *"This is my daughter, the heir to all of my troubles."* With that memory, a heaviness settled inside of me.

"It's so dark out here. I can't even tell where we are." I cleared my throat, needing a distraction. Memories. For years the only wish I had was for some of my memories to return, my memories from home, which seemed as murky as the air around us. Yet, with remembrance came pain.

"We'll be there soon." River glanced at me, meeting my eyes.

"Do you go into town often?"

"Sometimes. When I'm meeting someone."

"Like for a date?"

"Could be a date."

"Hm." I swallowed and looked away momentarily. "Do you normally bring your dates back to the house? I can't imagine what that must be like when the tide is high."

"We have boats." His eyes twinkled.

"They say this water is angry. I'm not really sure I'd ever get on a boat."

"I'm sure you would in the right circumstance."

"Why are you selling?" I asked suddenly. The car began its track up the winding hill and I needed to take my mind off the idea that we could go overboard anytime.

"I'm not sure that I am. I just want to know what my options are."

"Oh."

"My father is ill. My mother never did quite like this house. She's looking to move to the Italian countryside, someplace far."

"Oh." My brows rose. "Your mother . . . Sarah?"

"Stepmother. Yes." River's lips twitched. "She'd be happy to know she hasn't been forgotten."

"Forgotten?" I let out a laugh. "Legends never die."

"That's the truest thing I've heard in a long time."

I felt some of my anxiety ease a little. "So, your father is ill?"

"He is."

"What's wrong with him? If I may know."

"The doctors can't quite figure it out. They've run tests and scans and find nothing, yet he's lost weight, energy . . . " He looked forward.

My gaze followed. The only thing I could make out was the rocky path, which made the car bounce every so often.

My stomach clenched. I hoped I wouldn't throw up all the tequila I'd drunk. I'd never done it before, but there was a first time for everything. I just didn't want my first time to be in the back of a luxury car that probably cost what my shoes cost to detail. Suddenly, there was a low, and I knew we were finished going up the hill and getting closer to the house. I'd seen the picture I'd taken so many times, you'd think seeing it in person wouldn't be shocking, but it was. I'd hoped so much that being here would mean that my memories would come flooding back. That wasn't the case. I didn't remember seeing the house at all. It was so much bigger than I remembered. An estate. A dark, gray estate with decaying windowpanes. Even the trees on the property looked dead, but that could be because of the lack of grass. It was an impossibility, this house, yet there it was, staring right back at me.

"Is it really six miles from the gate to the house?" I asked.

"Six and a half."

"It feels farther."

"Distance is an illusion."

"Much like time."

"Much like time." He grinned.

My heart leaped. I focused on the trees to get a grip. There were no flowers, no leaves, just twirling branches on trunks.

"Do the trees ever flourish?"

"One does."

"One," I said. The magic tree. "So the rest are just . . . dead all the time?"

"Does anything ever truly die?"

"Yes." My father had just died and I saw him lying in a casket just one day ago, so definitely.

"I don't believe that."

"But you just said the trees don't flourish."

"That doesn't mean they're dead."

"Master River." That was the driver as he parked the car in front of the steps that led to the house and got out of the car, opening the door for River.

"Thank you, Gustavo." River got out of the car.

I stayed in my seat, not just because I knew one of them would open the door for me, but because I truly was regretting all of this. Suddenly, one night in jail didn't seem so bad after all, but then River opened the door and offered me his hand and looked at me with those dark eyes of his and I just took it.

CHAPTER NINE

I STARED AT THE EXTERIOR OF THE HOUSE AS RIVER WALKED UP THE steps. It was paneled in dark gray and had a porch that wrapped around its entirety. The house had such an eerie feel to it and I hadn't even stepped inside yet. I wasn't sure I wanted to. The more I looked at it, the less comfortable I felt. An uneasy feeling spread through me. For me to have taken a picture of the house, the picture I took and published and sold, I would have had to be standing just a few feet from it, but that was impossible. Nowadays, I could say it was my lens, but I didn't have the lenses I had now, then. I willed myself to remember, but couldn't, and it was madness.

"Are you going to stare at it all night?" River asked.

I blinked and made my way up the stairs. The porch was filled with black rocking chairs that swayed with a creak as the wind picked up. I shivered and rushed up the rest of the steps.

When I reached River, I expected him to open the door. Instead, he cleared his throat and the large double doors before us opened. A pale woman with dark hair, dressed in a black blouse and long black skirt that seemed too long for her not to trip on, was on the other side. She didn't smile, didn't welcome me, didn't even acknowledge me. She kept her head slightly bowed and moved out of the way for us to walk inside. There was music playing. Old music, the kind you play at a cocktail hour so that people can stand around and talk over it. As we walked farther into the house and I took in the dimly lit hallway and the hall full of mirrors, I wondered if I'd stepped into another century, another lifetime. It felt stuffy inside the house, but then we reached the foyer and it opened up to a party, which changed the mood of the house. It wasn't that it was light in this area, but everything was vibrant; the people were talking and laughing and drinking and dancing. Everyone was in costume, all black, feathers everywhere. It was . . . oddly cool.

"Master River, your bed has been downturned," the woman said beside us, her voice low and meek.

"Thank you, Mayra." River walked toward the people with such an air of importance, that I found myself falling behind until he glanced over his shoulder and looked at me. "Miss Guzman will be staying here tonight. Maybe for the remainder of the week."

"The remainder of the week?" I rushed forward. "I didn't agree to that. You said one night."

"I know what I said, and you're free to go tomorrow morning," he said. I breathed out. "That doesn't mean I won't choose you again and have you right back here."

"Why would you . . ." I swallowed, my heart soaring into my throat. "Why would you pick me twice?"

"Why wouldn't I?"

"Do you want the long version or the short?"

"We already went over all the versions I'm interested in discussing and my answer has not changed nor will it."

I glanced over at Mayra, who was still standing there. She was staring at me, and what I saw in her eyes was pure, unfiltered hatred, before she turned her face away. The uneasy feeling inside me grew, an ivy that wrapped around my innards and held tight.

"Where will Miss Guzman be staying?" Mayra asked, her eyes still cast at the floor.

"My bedroom."

"She . . ." Mayra's head snapped up, her mouth growing tight. "What will Doña Sarah say? And Don Wilfredo?"

"I personally don't care what either of them have to say about it."

"Very well." She swallowed and took a step back. "Does Miss Guzman have luggage?"

"She does not. I'll need Gustavo to bring her a trunk. Now, if you'll excuse us, we have a party to attend." River offered me his arm. I put mine in it reluctantly.

"Sure thing." Mayra bowed and walked away, disappearing into a dark hallway on the other side.

"I . . . I need to use the restroom," I said.

"Again?" He raised an eyebrow.

"Yes."

He escorted me to a door. "I'll be nearby."

"Okay." I set my hand on the round doorknob.

"I trust that you know you can't go anywhere tonight." He shot me a look. "You're staying with me."

"I already agreed to." I jutted my chin up. "It doesn't mean I want to."

"That's funny, I don't remember asking your opinion."

I rolled my eyes and opened the bathroom door. It was either that or slap the arrogance off him. I shut it behind me and was grateful to find the light already on, though upon further investigation I realized the light was coming from two gas lamps. The bathroom itself was small, only a toilet and a sink with a mirror. The entire thing was tiled in black and white squares, from floor to ceiling, giving it a trippy appearance. I did my business, flushed the toilet, and started washing my hands, concentrating on the soap as I rinsed it off. When I looked up at my reflection, there was a dark figure behind me. I gasped, turning around quickly, but there was nothing there. I blinked, and blinked, and nothing. My heart pumped harder. I dried my hands quickly and left the bathroom in such a hurry, I ran into someone.

"I am—"

"Never mind." It was Mayra. I'd never seen anyone with such hollowed eyes. "Sir River awaits you."

"Yes." I blinked away from her and looked at the crowd of people in search of him.

When I found him, I walked over. He had a drink in his hand that he was lowering as he looked over at me, at the necklace I wore around my neck, a gift from my grandmother. One of the many that I wore but didn't necessarily believe in.

"Saint Olga, the saint of all widows." He hid a small smile behind a glass of scotch. "You have to hand it to the Catholic Church for not bothering to hide their sinners' pasts before idolizing them."

"You're saying you wouldn't have done the same in her shoes?" Those around us seemed to vanish as I met his gaze outright. "You wouldn't take revenge on someone for murdering your spouse?"

"I take plenty revenge," he said, still amused. "And yet, no one has idolized me for it."

"Give it time." I licked my lips. "You're not dead yet."

At that, River laughed a loud, throw-your-head-back laugh that seemed to shake the house in its wake. I could swear the lights flickered. I could swear I heard it sigh. I could swear a lot of things, but my attention was solely on him, on this gorgeous man who felt akin to sunlight on a gloomy day when he laughed. The party livened. The music was a little louder now and had switched to an upbeat Harry Belafonte. People started dancing, making circles and loops around us as we stood smack in the center of the foyer. River was no longer laughing, but he still looked just as amused as he watched me.

"I don't think it's funny," I said after a moment.

"You don't think what's funny?"

"Any of this and I don't appreciate you making fun of my necklace."

"Noted." He grinned. "I won't make fun of your necklace again."

"Do you dance?" I glanced at the people around us.

"Only with beautiful women."

"Oh." I bit my lip.

"Do you dance?"

"Only with handsome men."

"Well, then, you're in luck." He set down his now empty glass on the table beside him and closed the distance between us, offering me his hand.

"I didn't say you were handsome." I put my hand in his.

"You didn't have to."

"You just assume everyone thinks you're handsome?"

"I just assume people who look at me the way you do, like it's a struggle to look away, think I am."

I rolled my eyes. "So arrogant."

"Rightfully so, some would say."

"Hm." We started dancing, but as we started the song changed again, from salsa to more of a waltz. "This deejay has an interesting way of mixing music."

"He reads the room." River's voice was much closer now, in my ear.

"Your house is haunted."

"Oh? You saw a ghost?"

"I saw something in the bathroom. Something dark. Like smoke."

"And? Did you ask what it was?"

"No, obviously not." I pulled back slightly and looked up at him. "Do you talk to smoke?"

"If it appears to me."

I eyed him closely, but shook my head when he didn't give anything else away. He held me tighter, one hand on my back, the other in mine, and there was no room for me to inspect his eyes any longer because for now, at least, I was lost to this dance, to the way it felt to be held by him.

CHAPTER TEN

PEOPLE BEGAN LEAVING THE PARTY, BUT BEFORE THEY WERE ALL gone, River was pulling me toward the winding staircase that reminded me of *Gone with the Wind*. My house growing up had been big, but this was something else. This was a real mansion. The floors were white and black tiles, and the stairs were covered in a red carpet. I followed River, taking one step behind him. Something out of my left eye caught my attention and when I looked down between the spindles, I saw Mayra standing there, watching me with that same hateful expression on her face. I let out a gasp and sped up, bumping into River, who stopped walking and turned to me.

"What . . . " He glanced out to the foyer, and I looked with him, but Mayra was gone. "What happened?"

"She was just there," I managed when we finally reached the top of the staircase. "Mayra. She was just there staring at me."

"Don't mind her."

"She doesn't like me," I whispered. "And it makes me uneasy, the way she looks at me."

River didn't offer any more words of encouragement or try to placate me. He merely made a right when we reached the top and walked down another great hall. The wallpaper was different up here, but was also very much flower driven and dated. At the end of the hall, there was a door with a gold handle in the middle, which he turned and opened, waiting so that I would walk inside first. I did, tentatively.

"You're already here." He chuckled. "No use in acting timid now."

"I'm not acting timid." My eyes narrowed. "I'm nervous."

"Fair enough." He shut the door behind us.

I turned to look at the room. It looked like something that tourists would walk through in a museum. There was a four-poster bed in the middle of the room, with a fireplace in front of it. The walls in here were black it seemed, and it too was lit with oil lamps all throughout.

"I feel like I'm living in a black and white movie," I said, to which River laughed, but it was tight and not as amused.

The only thing that was light in the entire room was the bed, with a plush white comforter folded and white sheets. The four poles were connected by a white sheer fabric, a *mosquitero* to keep the bugs away, and I wondered if he slept with his windows open or didn't have air-conditioning. I would die without air-conditioning. It wasn't hot in here, not really, but I knew the moment my head hit the pillow I'd start kicking off all the sheets. That gave me pause. He hadn't brought me here to sleep. He'd brought me to sleep *with*. God knew I could do a lot worse than River Caliban. He was one of those rare men who was attractive to anyone who laid eyes on him. Yet, he was older, experienced, and I wasn't. I was just a ball of nerves. Maybe after a shower. Maybe if I gathered my wits. A warm shower always helped me do that.

"Will I be able to shower?" I turned to River.

"Of course." He walked over to where I assumed the bathroom was.

We walked past a sitting area with a daybed and two armchairs. It seemed to be tucked into the wall and also had a fabric that could serve as a privacy shield. It was such a strange thing to have in a bedroom, but then, I had to remind myself, this was the Caliban House. The bathroom was nice, considering. It had a his and hers sink and mirror and seemed to have more light than the rest of the house, but that wasn't saying much. There was a white clawfoot tub to the left and a shower to the right.

"I'm surprised you have a shower."

"Are you insinuating I'm dirty?" He raised an eyebrow.

"No, not at all, that's not what I—"

"Relax, Penelope. I was joking. I'm actually not a complete bore."

I swallowed and smiled slightly, hoping it looked somewhat grateful, which I was. After all, he hadn't raped, tortured, or killed me . . . yet.

"I'll get you a towel and some things for you to sleep in. Tomorrow morning, you'll be able to take photographs of the house."

"Thank you. Is it always this dark in here?"

River tilted his head slightly. "Most of the time. It should be better in the morning."

"I thought it was supposed to be light this week, for Carnival."

"Because of the tide?"

I nodded.

"The fog and darkness have nothing to do with the low tide." His eyes speared into mine as he said the words and I thought of my family, of our families. Of the curse. No. I shook my head. The curse was bullshit.

"I'll have my shower now. Thank you." I smiled again.

"Sure thing." He gave a nod and stepped out of the bathroom momentarily, only coming back to bring the towel and clothes he promised.

I shut the door behind him and locked it when he stepped out the second time and got to undressing quickly. Once I was under the head of the shower, with the light spray that felt like rain trickling over me, I shut my eyes, but then I saw Mayra with her anger, glaring at me. I gasped, opening my eyes again. There was nothing there. I looked over my shoulder and once again confirmed that there was nothing there. My heart pounded, clearly not getting the memo. I showered quickly, dried off quickly, and changed quickly into a long T-shirt and boxer briefs. The T-shirt was white and even though it wasn't completely see-through, I knew one gust of wind would have my nipples on display. It didn't matter. I had a say in this; I was given a choice, and I chose this. I chose to be here. I sealed my fate by going to Carnival, as River had said. With that thought, I stepped into the bedroom. He was standing in the middle of the room, staring at a painting of boats on an angry ocean.

"Your ships?" I asked.

"Something like that." He glanced over his shoulder. "The water was okay?"

FABLES & OTHER LIES

"Yes, actually."

"I hope you don't mind me showering. I also need to wash off the night. I think I have some glitter on me."

I nodded. I didn't see any glitter on him, but I liked the idea of privacy in this room.

"Make yourself at home." He signaled around the room, and bed.

I watched as he walked into the bathroom and shut the door. Only then did I let out a breath. Just looking at the bed made me sleepy. I walked over to it, stretching my feet with each step I took, and climbed in. It smelled manly. I inhaled deeply, closing my eyes as I tried to figure out the scent. It had the faint smell of cologne and cocoa butter. An interesting mix, but it was good, so good. I lay my head on the pillow and let out a quiet complaint. It was hard, like the bed. I couldn't imagine being comfortable in it, but then, my comfort wasn't what he'd brought me here for, was it? I hadn't really thought much about what would happen next. Would he walk out of the bathroom naked? Ready to have his way with me? Would he let me be? That was doubtful. He'd said I was to spend the night with him and men didn't say that unless they were talking about sex.

Everyone I knew—men and women alike—were into hooking up on the first night. Most of them were on apps that were solely used for hooking up. I was what people liked to call a prude. It wasn't that I wasn't comfortable in my skin, I was, but I suffered from acute paranoia, at least that was what I liked to call it. I was a big overthinker, and unfortunately, sex was one of the things I played out in my head a million times before actually doing it, which meant I never actually did it. It just wasn't on the top of my list of things I needed to do, that was all. As I lay there, thinking about all of the things that could go wrong—what if he didn't use a condom? What if the condom broke? I swallowed back an uneasy feeling. None of that would happen and I'd been a stickler about getting birth control shots for years. Not that birth control shots would help me from an STD. I took a deep breath and then another. I needed to calm down. I waited and waited, staring into the dim room, but River never seemed to come out of the bathroom. I wasn't sure how long I'd been waiting, but when I felt my eyes grow tired and yawned a sixth time, I succumbed to sleep.

Somehow, I knew I was dreaming. Maybe because I wasn't in the Caliban Manor, but my own little beach house on Amelia Island. I opened my eyes and saw my room, with the all-white walls and windows throughout. My pillow was plush underneath my head and when I inhaled I expected to smell the salt from the ocean just outside the windows, but instead, it was a man's cologne and cocoa butter I smelled. It pulled me back. River. As if I'd beckoned him with my thoughts, he appeared beside me, and even though I knew this wasn't real, I gasped. He was shirtless, his muscular arms and etched abs on full display as he propped his head on his hand. He had that sexy grin on his face, the one that made my heart palpitate uncontrollably. He reached out and caressed my bare skin, his fingers moving slowly along the dip of my hip, up to my breast, where he paused, his gaze still on mine.

"What are you doing?" I whispered, even though it was a dumb question.

"What you want me to do." His hand cupped my breast, his thumb rubbing over my nipple. Desire flooded through me, pooling in between my legs. "When was the last time you did this, little witch?"

"I don't know." I bit my lip to keep from moaning when he pinched my nipple, but it was futile; the moan ripped through me loudly as my head fell back.

His touch left my breast, exploring lower, until he reached my abdomen, and snaked his hand between my legs, two fingers running along my lips. I let out a shaky breath.

"Have you ever done this before?" His brows pulled in slightly. I shook my head. "How can that be?" His fingers moved in and out, in and out. He wasn't inside of me, yet I felt him everywhere. My heart felt like it might give out from pounding so hard.

"I just haven't."

"How can that be?" he asked again.

"I don't know." My voice was shaky, breathless.

If I thought my admission would make him ease up, I was wrong. He brought his head closer to me. My heart stopped. My lips parted. He didn't kiss me though, he ducked his head and licked the nipple he'd touched once, twice, three times, closing his mouth around it as his fingers continued to move slowly between my folds. I cried out, threw my head back, and shouted something, I couldn't be sure what. Something inside of me snapped and when he moved his mouth to my other nipple and continued to move his fingers, I felt myself grow impossibly wet between my legs and cried out his name in a chant.

River.

River.

River.

I was still panting, eyes closed, when I came to, but when I opened my eyes I wasn't in my little white cottage, but a dark bedroom. I gasped, sitting up in bed, holding the sheets to my chest. I looked around, but saw nothing. When I looked beside me, I saw River lying there, fast asleep. He wasn't naked. I could see that much. I held a hand over my heart and willed it to calm down. Nothing had happened. It was a dream. A very, very vivid dream. As I lay back down on my pillow, River stirred.

"You're entirely too wound up, little witch," he mumbled.

"Stop calling me that," I said, despite my quickening pulse.

"We have a long day ahead of us." He shifted in bed and turned to face me, his face incredibly close to mine. His lips turned up slightly. "You should get some rest."

I swallowed, nodding, and turned over to face the other way. I couldn't be sure, but he looked like he knew what I'd just imagined, dreamt. That was impossible, right? I forced myself to breathe normally. It was impossible.

CHAPTER ELEVEN

THERE WAS A LOUD KNOCK ON THE DOOR. THAT WAS HOW I woke up a second time. I quickly looked beside me to find River was no longer there. Somehow, that made me breathe a little easier. The dream was still replaying in my mind, not just the dream though, it was everything. My body seemed to be on fire from it. My breasts, between my legs. Everything felt as though it had happened. *Had it?* The knock on the door came again. I cleared my throat, but before I could invite them in, the door swung open and Gustavo appeared, rolling a large brown designer trunk behind him. He let it fall with a thump and looked up at me. Even in the daylight, he looked menacing, with an oversized frame that made him look like he was wearing shoulder pads underneath his suit.

"Good morning, ma'am." He nodded. "Mr. Caliban asked

me to bring this to you. I apologize that it took this long, but I trust the clothes are in your size."

"How would . . . did you just guess my size?"

"Size six. Is that suitable?" he asked, but before I could respond, he looked down at the trunk, which had a paper tucked into the side that said 4/6. He looked at me. "There are also size 4 pieces inside."

"That should be fine," I said, my voice coming out slower than I intended. "I won't be needing all of it." I studied Gustavo, who seemed to have no reaction to this. "Do you just keep trunks of different sized clothes here just in case a woman stays over?"

"I assure you, Mr. Caliban does his due diligence when it comes to his guests, as he likes to make sure they are well taken care of. Will you be needing anything else?"

"No. That should be fine." I licked my lips. "Where is River?"

"Mr. Caliban is busy in the study. Once you are ready, you may head downstairs. I'm told you will be taking photographs of the house today."

"That's correct."

"Oh. Before I forget." He walked outside again and was carrying two large canvas bags when he stepped back inside. He deposited them beside the trunk. "These are toiletries."

"Thank you."

"Will that be all?"

"Yes. I think you've covered it." I smiled gratefully.

He didn't.

He left the room and shut the door behind him without another word. I scrambled out of bed and walked over to the trunk, setting my hand over the leather. My mother had a similar trunk. It had been a gift from Papi from one of his many trips to Paris. Growing up, I could never be quite sure why a mattress and plastics manufacturer traveled so much, but as I got older and visited him at the factories, I understood that they relied on outside resources for materials. Most of my life I'd been told I'd inherit those companies, something that after I left I knew would be improbable, and then years later, when my mother called me one day and told me my father had sold the company to another family and handed out severance checks to longtime employees who had decided to quit, I mourned.

I never wanted the companies, but for some reason it hurt me that he trusted someone else with something that had been handed down to him and not his own daughter. Part of me thought it was because I wasn't a man. If I'd been a man, I was sure I wouldn't have been humiliated or kicked out of the house or banished. If I'd been a man, my father would have been proud. But I wasn't a man. I was just a woman with a problem between her legs.

The latch of the trunk was tight, as if it had never been opened, but I managed to pry it. What I found inside made me fall on my ass. Literally. Well taken care of was one thing, this was . . . a lot. There was a diamond necklace that looked like something only the Queen of England would have in her armory, set over a silk red fabric that glistened in the little light reflected in the room. I'd never worn a necklace like this. I wasn't sure I wanted the responsibility of one. I could barely bring myself to set it aside to look through the rest of it, but I managed to pick up the silk and set it on the floor beside me carefully before going back to the trunk. The first thing was a dark red dress. I stood, the red silk of the dress, so similar to the fabric on which the necklace was on, hit my forearms as it fell open. It was exquisite. Again, something unlike anything I'd ever worn before.

I was a skinny jeans and Converse or sandals kind of girl, combat boots when I felt like I needed an extra kick in my step. I didn't do jewels or fancy dresses or heels, much to my mother's dismay. The dress hung low between the breasts and the back was exposed. It was long and had a slight train. Just looking at it made my pulse quicken. Would I wear this to the gala? Was that what River intended? Would I stay? Would he actually drag me back here tonight as he'd said? I kind of wanted to find out. Maybe it was because I'd never been the person people chased after. Maybe it was because the idea of someone like River—handsome, rich, powerful—going out of his way to look for me was thrilling.

I recalled the memory of my dream, so vivid, so scandalous, unlike anything I'd ever experienced. The mere thought of it made me blush. My grandmother would be so ashamed. According to her, sex was something you waited for a husband to experience with. Even in a dream it was wrong. Even unwilled. She'd probably make me drink one of her concoctions to drive the Devil out of me and make me pray twelve Hail Marys. I set the dress down on the bed and went back to the trunk. The rest was more casual—beige trousers, beige and white button-down shirts, white T-shirts, black loafers, different color cardigans. It was all very classic, very Audrey Hepburn-esque. I would probably never buy myself any of this, but I found that I actually loved it. There were underwear and bras in one section of the trunk, differing sizes, so I knew they hadn't been spying on me or anything. It was all very delicate yet sexy. Lace and pearls and mesh that once again was unlike anything I owned. The pajamas were also made of silk, pants and button-downs that I'd only seen in magazines.

I grabbed what I would wear now and set aside the rest inside the trunk, placing each piece the way I'd found it, neatly folded and compartmentalized. When I was finished getting ready, I looked at myself in the mirror. The lighting in this bathroom was atrocious, but even still, I felt pretty. I felt . . . classy in my preppy beige outfit. Instead of putting on the cardigan, I tied it around my neck and headed out of the room, feeling like a tennis mom on her way to pick up her children. As I stepped outside of the room and shut the door quietly behind me, I froze. Mayra was standing across from me, looking like she'd been here for hours. Her dark eyes gave me a full sweep.

"I see you've helped yourself to the clothing."

"Only upon your boss's insistence." I stared right back, despite the fact that my heart was pounding in my ears.

"You don't belong here. I hope you know that." Her gaze narrowed. "But I guess we'll have to entertain ourselves with your measly presence while you're here."

"Measly." I huffed out a laugh, shaking my head. Now I was annoyed. "Is there a reason you're here right now?"

"Sir River would like me to escort you to his office." She turned around and started walking quickly.

I followed at a more leisurely pace. I figured if I got lost, I got lost, but I wasn't about to play this woman's stupid games. We seemed to walk down many corridors before we reached the winding staircase. It was definitely not the route we'd taken upstairs and I knew she'd meant to make things difficult for me. When we reached large wooden double doors, she stopped walking and set a hand out to open them.

"Sir, your guest has arrived," she announced, stepping inside and waiting for me to step in behind her.

I blinked. When she said a study, I'd expected a room with a desk, not a huge library with a dome ceiling. Like the rest of the house, it looked . . . old. Decaying, with wallpaper that had come off in some sections and gold that was rusted on the chandelier. I couldn't understand why a family with so much money would let this house fall apart like this.

"Thank you, Mayra. That'll be all," River said, breaking into my thoughts. I blinked and looked at him before my attention turned to Mayra who was staring at me.

"I'm sure I'll be seeing you around." Her smile didn't reach her eyes when she looked at me right before turning to leave the room.

"Interesting *study*." I looked at him, finally. He was sitting behind the desk, dressed in a white button-down with the sleeves folded up.

He had a classic look about him, an old Hollywood star kind of look, with his naturally golden skin, head full of dark hair with that side part, and perfect bone structure. He could play the lead in any film. I thought of the dream again and felt my heart beat a little faster. It had been a dream. A dream that I conjured. I blinked away from my thoughts when I realized he was still staring at me, as if waiting for me to add on to my previous statement.

"What's interesting about the study?"

"All of it. The ceiling, the grandeur." I looked at the large colorful stained-glass window behind him. It looked like something that belonged in a basilica, not a home. "The window is especially beautiful."

"It is, isn't it?" He turned in his chair and looked at it. "A gift from the Pope."

"The Pope?" I blinked. "Which one?"

"One of the Piuses. I always get them confused."

"I've never seen this particular image." I walked forward, around the desk and tilted my head to look at the window up close. "It's . . . different."

The glass had clear and yellows, and blues and grays and showed the typical rendition of Our Lady of Charity holding a baby and ascending into the clouds as a shipwreck took place in turbulent waters beneath her. *A gift from the Pope.* I shook my head. Wela would be beside herself if she was in the mere presence of something like this, knowing its origin.

"A gift for what?" I glanced over my shoulder. River's dark eyes were on mine, as if he'd been watching me the entire time, even though I'd been turned around.

"A gift for a curse."

"What do you mean?"

"How much do you know about my family?"

"Enough to know I shouldn't be here."

"Didn't you take the most famous photograph ever taken of the house?" He raised an eyebrow. "Why didn't you heed those warnings then?"

I felt myself cower a little. I'd defended having that picture to myself, to my parents, to my family, but I was at a loss for words when it came to someone of the actual Caliban family. I mean, I'd profited a lot from that photograph and technically I had no right to it, and that was just the tip of the iceberg when it came to that subject. I focused on taking pictures of the sand. Finally, I thought, fuck it, and met his eyes again.

"Are you offended?"

"Why would I be offended?" He crossed his arms. "I

mean, besides the fact that you trespassed private property and took a picture of one of the most sought-after homes in the world and then profited off of it and didn't even think to ask our permission before doing so."

"Ouch." I tore my gaze away from his and looked at the window again. None of what he'd said was wrong, and what was I supposed to say? That I didn't remember taking the picture at all?

"It's in the past."

"And yet you bring it up in such detailed form." I took and let out a breath before meeting his eyes again. "Was that why you chose me? Is that why you want me here? To ridicule me?"

"Have I ridiculed you?"

"No."

"Then there's your answer."

"Not really. Not at all." I felt my frown deepen and decided to let bygones be bygones. "I'd like to take the pictures now."

"Before you've had breakfast?"

"I'd like to take advantage of the light." I looked at the window again, shaking my head. Light had just been seeping through and was no longer.

"Isn't that what technology is for? I assume you'll be able to brighten the images."

"Well, yeah, but why would I?" I walked back to the door, taking my camera out and uncapping the lens as I did. I turned to face the room and raised the camera, pointing the lens in his direction. I snapped a picture, then another, getting a full angle of the room. I'd just have to photoshop him out.

"There you go taking pictures without permission again."

He stood up and walked around the desk to join me. He smelled like his bed, like some manly cologne that I wanted to drown in.

"Will you leave the furniture?" I snapped a picture, then another.

"I believe so. I can't imagine it fitting into any new house."

I nodded. River escorted me out of the study and walked me down the hall toward the front door. "Are you sure you don't want breakfast first?"

"I'm positive. Thanks." I glanced over at him. "Did you have breakfast?"

"It would have been rude to eat without my guest."

"Oh." I lowered the camera and let the strap hang from my neck. "I guess I can take some coffee."

He didn't smile, not with his mouth, but his eyes lit up. He made a right before we were all the way to the door and walked me to the dining room.

CHAPTER TWELVE

I STOPPED AT THE THRESHOLD. THE TABLE SAT TWENTY, MAYBE thirty, people easily, and it was set for a feast. There were only two place settings though, on the right side of the table, across from each other.

"This is just for us?" I looked up at River, wide-eyed.

"We don't have guests often, so the staff likes to make a show of it when we do."

"Wow." I walked over to one of the chairs, touching the top of the intricate wooden design. The upholstery looked dated, with an ivory fabric and pink flowers, but the wood was intact and seemed to have gold on the edges.

"They were imported from Italy." River walked to the chair across from me, setting a hand on it as he watched me. I realized he was waiting for me to sit down first, and once I did, he followed suit. There were three silver warming dishes and two bread baskets. If I wasn't hungry before, I definitely was now.

"Help yourself," he said.

"Thanks." I smiled and stood with my plate, leaning over to open the first silver dish.

It was filled to the top with salami. It was an exaggeration of food. I took two pieces, shut it, and moved on to the next one as River traced my steps and served himself. There were poached eggs and fried eggs. I took one fried egg and some mashed plantains, then served myself coffee and dumped creamer and sugar in it.

"What do you do with the leftovers?" I stirred the coffee.

"The staff eats it."

"They haven't had food?" I stopped stirring.

"They eat after we eat."

"No wonder they're so mean."

"Mean?"

"Mayra has been plotting my death from the moment I walked in here."

"Is that so?" He smiled, but it wasn't kind and did nothing to dismiss my fear.

"I want to leave after I take the pictures."

"Why would you want to leave?" He met my gaze, seemingly puzzled by this.

"I'm supposed to meet my friends for drinks."

"Your friends will be here later tonight. Why not just enjoy the festivities and leave with them?"

"I'd rather not wait until then."

"Do you feel uneasy here?" His brows pulled in slightly. "Is it Mayra? I can dismiss her."

"You'd dismiss someone on your staff for me?" I blinked,

shaking my head. "No. That's . . . that would be awful. And it's not her."

Not *just her*, I wanted to say, but didn't. River didn't argue anymore. We finished eating in peace and he showed me the areas I could photograph.

"It's so very . . . antiquated," I said, sitting down on a bench across from the staircase to scroll through the photos I'd taken. Some of the wings were off-limits, but these would do. He sat beside me and looked over my shoulder as I scrolled.

"Not your style?"

"I'm not sure what my style is yet when it comes to home decoration. I'm renting for now and the house came fully furnished." I clicked to the next one, of one of the six sitting rooms; this particular one was dark purple, all purple walls, all purple furniture, all purple carpet. "But this is definitely not my style."

"Is your style more of a small house with a modern feel? On the water?"

My face whipped up, heart slamming. "How do you know that?"

"Know what?"

"About my house."

"I don't. I'm assuming, asking you a question." He cocked his head. "Most people from islands tend to gravitate to the water. It has quite a pull on us, don't you think?"

"Oh. Well, I live on Amelia Island, right on the water. For now, anyway, so I guess maybe you're onto something."

"For now? Where will you live forever?"

"I'm not sure." I looked back at the pictures. "Maybe there. Maybe Europe. Not on the water."

"That's not likely."

"Based on your assumptions." I felt myself smile. "What do you do anyway? Do you work? Did you go to school? Have a life? Are you just a trust-fund baby living a trust-fund-baby life?"

"Not much of a baby." He let out a laugh. He wasn't wrong. I didn't want to ask how old he was, but I assumed much closer to thirty than I was. "I'm thirty-two," he said, as if reading my mind.

"Oh. Wow. And you don't want a wife or a family?" I frowned.

"Do you think someone would want me as a husband?"

"Uh, yes."

He grinned at that.

"I mean, just based on all of the awful human beings who end up with families, I mean," I said, "not that you're an awful human being at all."

River chuckled, his eyes dancing.

"What I mean is, I think there's someone out there for everyone." I glanced away to hide my fierce blush, knowing that all the makeup in the world or my olive complexion wouldn't cover it.

"I agree. I think there's someone for everyone," he said. "I wouldn't call myself a trust-fund baby, but I guess for the sake of keeping things simple, I am in the family business. I have things that I do for fun, for fulfillment, if you will."

"Oh." I raised an eyebrow. "What do you do that's fulfilling?"

"You ask a lot of questions." He tore his gaze away from mine.

I followed it and saw that Mayra was standing on the

other side of the staircase, right at the entrance of the hallway that River didn't allow me to walk through to photograph. She was just staring at us. I swallowed, hating the uneasiness her presence brought. Was she a past lover of River's? Was that why she hated me so much? Because truly, she could have him. No man was worth that kind of trouble or hatred.

"Ignore her." River looked at me, pulling my attention from Mayra. I glanced over at her one more time, but she was gone.

I let out a breath. "Why does she hate me so much? Is she an ex of yours?"

"No."

"Someone you sleep with but don't take seriously?" My heart stopped beating for a second, as if anticipating the pain his answer might bring.

"So many questions." His mouth twitched. "Come on, I'll show you outside and then drive you back to Pan."

When we walked toward the door and he opened it, I felt myself breathe a little easier. He wasn't holding me hostage after all. The fog seemed to have lifted. When I looked up at the sky, I couldn't see the sun, but the sky was mostly clear, which was unexpected. I looked out into the distance, fully expecting to see some sign of water, but there was none of that either. It was as though it had disappeared completely. I couldn't help it, I walked down the steps quickly and onto the lawn. The grass was impossibly green, not covered in dark sand as I'd expected it to be. I looked at the tree I'd seen last night and saw that it had green leaves covering every branch.

"Impossible." I walked over to the tree and stared.

"Isn't that what life is? A series of impossibilities." River walked up beside me. I shook my head, mouth hanging open, and looked up at him.

"But how?"

"They call it the Tree of Life." He tucked his hands into his pockets. "Some say it can cure anything. Others say it can curse anything. I guess like all sources of power, it depends on how you use it."

"Do you believe that?" I looked between him and the tree before settling on him.

"I've seen it work."

"Why not use the leaves to heal your father then? Didn't you say he's ill?"

"You assume he wants to be healed."

I frowned. "Wouldn't anyone who's ill want to be healed?"

"My father has lived a long, fulfilling life. He's been ready to transcend for quite some time."

"But . . . in theory, if he were to eat some leaves or drink a tea or whatever, he'd live longer?"

"If he wants to."

"What do you mean if he wants to?"

"If he drinks a tea with the leaves he would probably just forget the pain he's in. It wouldn't prolong his impending death."

"Why not?"

"Because it's not what he wants. Not really anyway." He brought his hands out of his pockets, running his fingers through his hair with one. "People think they know what they want, but they don't. It's been proven time and time again. A poor person prays for a fortune, gets said fortune, and remains unhappy." He shrugged. "Humans are the same across the board. Always unhappy. Always searching for more. Never satisfied with what they have."

"And then we die," I said.

"And then they die." He smiled.

"I didn't even know witches could die." I glanced back at the house. It was beautiful, despite its darkness.

"Who says they can?"

"Is your father a witch?"

River chuckled. "Was yours?"

I pursed my lips at that. *Touché.* He laughed louder, that real, unfiltered laugh I witnessed last night. It truly was a beautiful sound. The fog lifted a little more, the clouds opening up just so, just a bit, so that the sun shone through. I looked up to see the single ray of sun breaking through the clouds. It took me a second to react, but when I did, I gathered my camera and started to take pictures of the house. I walked to the front and took some more. With the light, the green grass, and fruitful tree, it looked like a dream. A house with a wraparound porch to drink tea in on a hot summer day and a yard to run around.

"How many acres surround the house?" I snapped a picture of the flowers near my feet, not for the real estate company, or my blog, but because I was compelled to. They looked like pink dahlias.

"Ten acres." River walked over to me, standing beside me again. He kept looking over my shoulder to see the screen on my camera, which was something I normally couldn't stand people doing but I didn't mind when he did it. Besides, it was his house.

"Ten acres is a lot."

"You know this is an island, right?" He sounded amused. "We have about twenty-five thousand acres total, give or take."

My brows rose. "I mean, I guess there is no definition that says an island can't be just a dot as long as it's surrounded by water."

"Yes, that is the definition of an island, Penelope." He chuckled. "What I mean to say is that this is a piece of that island." He pointed in the direction of Pan. "A big chunk of it, too. Pan is what, two-hundred and forty miles long?"

"Something like that."

"They say originally, before the curse, before everything, there was no part between this and that and that the entire island measured two-hundred and eighty miles give or take."

"This doesn't seem like it would be forty miles." I looked around.

"You'd never know it because you're just in the entrance of it. We have miles and miles behind us, and restaurants and grocery stores and everything an inhabited island is supposed to have."

"What?" I blinked. "No way. Who lives here?"

"People."

I searched his eyes. He stared right back. It made sense. His staff had to come from somewhere. It was just that I always associated Dolos Island with the Caliban Manor and nothing else.

"How big is the house?"

"About fifteen thousand square feet."

"Wow," I whispered, stepping away, a little further now.

My feet wouldn't keep walking though, not even halfway to the black iron gates. Maybe it was because now I knew I'd have to go down that gravelly, winding road to get there, or because I was half expecting the water to flood back up. And what if it did and I was standing at the edge here? Worry rendered me motionless. What if the water came back? What if it covered us and we drowned here? I swallowed hard. What if that was my penance for my wish, for my success?

"You worry too much," River said, startling me.

"What?" I met his gaze.

"The water won't come. That's what you're worried about, isn't it?"

"How do you know it won't? How do you know a wave won't hit us and drown us?"

"Because I've stood here countless times and I've taken the drive to and from the house every year this week."

"And you just . . . trust that it won't happen?" I eyed his profile.

"I don't trust that it won't happen." River glanced over at me, a small smile tugging the side of his mouth.

My heart beat so quickly, I couldn't remember what it was I was worried about a second ago. I blinked away from his gaze and looked back again, toward where I knew the gates were; an expanse of nothingness covered it.

"Are you ready to go?" he asked after a moment.

"Yes." I followed him to the dark gray R8 that awaited us at the side of the house. "Why do you have such nice cars if you have nowhere to really drive them?"

"Who says I have nowhere to drive them?" He glanced at me once we were inside the car. I pulled my seatbelt on. He didn't.

"I don't know. I mean, I guess you can drive it around Dolos if it's such a developed island like you say it is." I shrugged.

"I drive in many places."

"Do you look forward to the party every year?"

"Not really. I'm not a fan of having strangers in my home." He shot me a look. "You're an exception."

I didn't want that statement to make me smile, but I couldn't help that it did. "You're about to let a lot of strangers into your house if you're serious about selling it."

"Nope."

"What do you mean nope?" I let out a laugh. "People will want to tour."

"People will do virtual tours. That's what you're here for."

"This isn't a video camera." I waved my camera.

"Photos will be enough."

"Not . . . that's not how this works, not for a house listed at fifteen million dollars."

"It'll have to be enough and because I'm sure you want this deal to go through as much as I do, I'm assuming you'll clean up the photographs and make them work. Surely you'll get a cut out of that as well."

I stared at him for a second, jaw twitching. He stared right back. For someone touting the whole *it's all in the past* thing, he sure had a sour attitude. A sour attitude that for some crazy reason I wanted to right. I didn't want him to see me the way he saw them. I wasn't like them.

"Look." I took a deep breath and tried again. "I know our families have a long history of . . . disdain."

"Disdain?" He scoffed. "Your family started a rumor that we were devil worshippers."

"And on behalf of them, I apologize for the inconvenience, but you don't seem to be doing badly. I mean, you own so much land outside of this one island. What more could you possibly want?"

"You'd be surprised at the things I want." His expression darkened when he said those words.

My heart dipped into my stomach. The dream flashed in my head again and I seemed to lose my train of thought for a moment. I blinked away from him and shook my head for good measure.

"What I'm saying is that I can't imagine being called names was that much of an inconvenience to a family like yours."

"It certainly wasn't an inconvenience to the Guzmans to have our name tarnished. Your family employs most of the island."

"Yours employed a lot of our family members." I felt my eyes narrow. "And some have disappeared."

"*One* disappeared."

"Oh, so you know about Esteban."

"I've heard of him. Were you close?"

"Yes." I jutted my chin away from him.

"Well, then, I'm sorry for your loss."

"Are you though?" I looked at him again. "My grandmother told me that your father never even let my family past the gates to check for themselves."

"My father could be a bit of a jerk in his day."

"A bit? Have you ever lost someone and had no body to grieve over and bury?" I let my camera swing, the weight of the motion scratching the back of my neck. "It's awful. An endless grieving process."

"I know." His voice was almost a whisper, but his words were clear.

Had it not been for the anguish that flashed in his eyes I'd have called his bluff. I swallowed the rest of my words instead. I hadn't come here to blame him for matters he couldn't help and had nothing to do with. Doing that would make me no better than any of my predecessors and I'd always said I was done with their games. I took a deep breath and exhaled, tilting my head up slightly to meet his gaze again.

"Let's call a truce. For now at least."

"For now?" His eyes danced. "Does that mean you still might use those combat boots you brought to kick me?"

"I forgot my boots." I gasped, turning in my seat.

"Do you want to go back?" He raised an eyebrow.

"No way. I'll just have Dee get them for me tonight." We were almost at the gate now and I was half scared of what might happen if we turned back now.

"So, you *do* mean to kick me with them?"

"Only if you make me."

"I might just have to." When he smiled, it was everything I'd been warned against. Devilish, seductive, terrifyingly alluring. He knew it, too. He knew he had me. He didn't make a show of it though, not the way all the boys my age would have. Instead, he parked the car in front of the iron gates and turned it off. "Shall we?"

"I have one more question." I got out of the car, as did he. He unlocked the gate for me and I realized Gustavo was standing on the other side with a group of men, guarding the general area.

"Yes?" River tilted his head as he walked me out of the gates and back to Pan Island.

"How did you know I'd be at Carnival?"

"Just a hunch."

"A hunch?" I frowned. "Did you look at the list of attendees?"

If he'd looked at the list he would have seen my name on it. We all had to sign in upon entering. Though I wasn't sure why anyone would bother to look at the list of names, and a list of names didn't include faces. Unless it did. I never saw the list.

"No."

"So, how'd you know I was there?"

He stared at me for a long, quiet moment. I felt every hair stand up, every nerve ending zap, before he finally looked away. My heart pounded erratically. River was good-looking, yes, but this was something else. This was . . . inexplicable.

"A hunch." He met my gaze again. "You should be ready by five-thirty. I'll send your dress with Gustavo."

"What? Send it where? I'm not even going to the party."

"Gustavo," River said loudly. "Let it be known that I'm choosing Penelope Guzman to accompany me tonight."

"Yes, sir."

"Do you dare defy the rules, Miss Guzman?" His eyes were dancing when he looked at me again.

My jaw dropped. It took me a second to gather my wits before I could respond, "I don't even know where I'll be. I'm not going back home and—"

"Tell Miss Dolly that you'll be needing the room upstairs. That should cover it."

I blinked. "I don't even . . . Dolly . . . I mean . . . "

"Penelope."

"What?"

"Go to Dolly's. Your friends are waiting for you." He brought a hand up and caressed my face. "I'll see you later."

With that he turned around and walked past the gate again. My mouth was still hanging open as I watched him get in the car and peel away. The only thing I could think was, *What the hell just happened?* And the only answer I could come up with was River Caliban. He happened.

CHAPTER THIRTEEN

WHEN I PULLED THE DOOR OPEN TO DOLLY'S BAR AND WALKED inside, all heads turned to me. Dee and Martín were sitting at our usual table, but before I headed there, I first walked over to Dolly, who was behind the bar.

"He told me," she said when I reached her. "I'll take you up in a minute. I'm sure you want to rest."

"I'm fine."

"Okay." She raised an eyebrow. "I already set your martini on the table over there."

I walked toward my friends. They were both wide-eyed, watching me as I slid into the booth across from them and took a hefty sip of the martini, coughing when the vodka hit me hard.

"First of all, who are you?" Dee asked.

"What?" I blinked.

"What are you wearing? You're dressed in . . . light colors?" She looked confused. "You look like you just stepped out of a Ralph Lauren commercial."

"Oh." I looked down at myself and laughed. "I kind of like it."

"It suits you." Dee folded her hands in front of her. "So, do tell."

"We didn't do anything. There was a small party when we got there and then we slept in the same bed, but did nothing, and he let me take pictures of part of the house this morning before driving me over here." I took another sip. "He also picked me again today."

"He picked you again?" Dee's brows rose.

"And all you did was sleep beside each other?" Martín's brows rose as well.

"Trust me, I don't understand it either. I feel like this is some kind of revenge scheme, but he's not . . . I mean, he hasn't done anything bad to me."

"Yet." Dee's mouth formed into a thin line.

"Yet," I agreed.

"What can he do?" Martín asked. "He seems perfectly fine."

"Too perfect," Dee said. "And he's from that island." She pulled a disgusted face.

"Technically, yes, but he's lived in London, France, Greece. It's not like the man isn't well traveled and is only stuck in one place," Martín said.

"How do you know?" I asked.

"I pay attention." Martín took a sip of his drink, his face reddening. "And I low-key stalk the Calibans."

"You have a crush on him or something?" Dee raised a questioning eyebrow.

"No, nothing like that. I just find them fascinating. They're the reason I started visiting Pan Island, to begin with. All of the legends and folklore."

"Oh, God." I groaned. "I hate what that picture did to this island."

"No offense, but the legends were well established before your photo surfaced or The Haunt became a thing."

"That actually makes me feel a little better." I finished off my drink. "So, what'd you learn about the Calibans?"

"Not much. Not much that I believe to be real anyway. I learned that the curse caused a literal rift, when what is now known as Dolos Island broke off from Pan Island."

"How did that happen?" I sat up straighter.

"What was the curse?" Dee asked.

"There are different accounts. Mostly I think the Guzmans didn't want the Calibans moving in on their land. The Guzmans were here first. They founded Pan Island. They owned the crops and were proud to have freed their people. When the Calibans moved in with their promises to be nice, they were given a chance, but it is said that they broke that promise."

"How?" I leaned forward. "What did they do?"

"They enslaved people again. Raped women. Impregnated them." Martín shot me a look. "Not that your people weren't doing the same to them, but obviously your people practically own this island to this day so the tours are very one-sided."

"None of this matters," Dee said. "You shouldn't feel bad for kissing a man who had as little to do with this as you did."

"We didn't kiss." I swallowed.

"But if you did, it wouldn't be terrible," Martín added.

"He's still a Caliban."

"And you're still a Guzman. I'm sorry to say but in most accounts I found outside of these tours, you're the bad guy."

"I'm not a guy." I raised an eyebrow. "Besides, like Dee said, I can't be crucified for the sins of those who came before me."

"But he can?"

"I'm not crucifying him."

"You may not be, but the town is. Last night, after you left, a slew of riots started."

"Is that true?" I looked at Dee.

"Let's just say, you don't want to go visit your grandmother right now." She bit her lip. "It died down quickly though."

"Oh my God." I buried my face in my hands. "Now they're going to think the worst of me even if I didn't do anything at all."

"I'd say."

I groaned.

"Penny, I'm ready for you." That was Dolly, smiling as she walked over.

"I have to go. I'll see you guys later."

"Will you be going to the party tonight then?" Dee asked.

"I mean." I shrugged. "I guess so."

"See you then." She smiled. "Don't worry, we're on your side."

I waved at them and followed Dolly to the back of the bar and then up a flight of stairs I'd never seen before. We walked up to the third floor and she gave me a set of keys.

"This is the only one I have, so you best not lose it."

"I won't." I looked at the keys and the only door on the floor before walking over and opening it. "Is this . . . his?"

"Yes, ma'am, it is." Dolly followed me inside, flipping the switch to the fan as we walked in. "It feels stuffy in here."

I paused by the door. It was everything the Manor was not. New. Or rather, restored, since I knew how old this building was. Still, the gray-washed hardwood floors and all-white furniture gave the entire place an airy feel to it. The walls were bare, and the ones that weren't had generic art on them, which I didn't peg River to have picked out.

"Does he come here often?"

"Often enough."

"How does he get here?" I turned to Dolly.

"However he wants, love." She laughed. "Helicopter, yacht, I don't know. The man has the means to travel, that's for sure."

"So why own this apartment on an island that doesn't even like him?"

"That's a question you'd have to ask him." She smiled a small smile that told me she knew the answer to that question but either wasn't at liberty to say or just didn't want to. "I'll let you know when Gustavo is here with your clothes for tonight's party."

"Are you going to the party?"

"Do I look crazy to you?" She shot me a pointed look from the door. "I wouldn't be caught dead on Dolos Island after dark."

"Why not?"

"I have my own demons to battle. I don't need to go to war with lost souls." She shut the door between us before I could ask any more questions.

I went over and locked it. I'd been on Dolos after dark and nothing happened. I shook my head. This was exactly why I didn't believe in any of the stories my grandmother told. As far as I was concerned, they were campfire stories. I busied myself looking around the apartment, trying to see if I could find anything that could give me a glimpse into River's life, but I came up short. When I got tired of searching, I went to the bedroom and got underneath the covers. I inhaled. The sheets smelled like him. It was faint, as if he hadn't been here in a while, but it was there, and I found myself shutting my eyes to see if I could memorize it. I had every intention of watching television, but instead, fell asleep.

It was dark out. I rushed behind Esteban.

"I can go home," I said.

"No. Just wait for me outside. I'll be quick."

I sighed heavily. "You said that last time and you took an hour."

"Well, P. You can't rush a woman's pleasure." He smiled over at me. I cringed.

"That's disgusting."

"You'll understand it one day." He wrapped an arm over my shoulder. "I'll show you."

"Show me what?" I pulled away from him.

"That it can be good."

"That's even more disgusting." I pulled a face. "You're my cousin."

"So is half this island. You think it's going to stop them?" He walked forward. "When your breasts start to grow more." He brought a hand up and grazed my breast before I could jump back.

"Stop. I'll tell on you if you keep talking like this."

"I'm just joking." He laughed. "Relax. You think I'd do

anything to you?" I kept my distance. He noticed and glared. "Just go home. You're acting like a baby today."

I turned around and did as I was told, not because I followed orders, but because I was scared. Scared of him, of what he'd do. It was dumb. I knew Esteban. He was more of a brother than a cousin to me. He wouldn't hurt me. Besides, my father would kill him if he did. He knew that. As I walked home, arms crossed, eyes on the unpaved road ahead, I heard something snap in the forest beside me. I gasped and stopped walking, looking over into the darkness. I couldn't see anything at all, but Esteban's words rang clear in my head. Would a man hurt me? Would they dare? I held myself tighter, willing myself to move, but for some reason I couldn't. I was near the iron gates, near the Devil's Chair, which I'd sworn I'd never sit on. The fog grew heavy around me and I began to shiver, still looking out into the forest. Another twig, and another, snapped, but still, there was nothing there. Then I saw two eyes, two golden eyes staring right at me. That was when I ran as fast as I could.

When I reached my house, I slammed the door shut behind me. Wela rushed over.

"I saw something. Yellow eyes. In the forest," I said, out of breath.

She gasped, doing the sign of the cross. "La Ciguapa."

"No." I frowned. "I don't think so. It didn't look like a witch. It was just eyes."

"A woman's eyes?"

"I don't know. How can eyes belong to either man or woman?"

"Did she have backward feet?" The question came from my father who'd walked into the room smoking a cigarette while I was speaking to my grandmother.

I frowned, looking up at him. My father didn't believe in childish tales, and as far as I was concerned, La Ciguapa was a childish tale. A folktale people told to keep their children or straying husbands home at night.

"I don't think it was a woman at all," I said finally.

"I'll make you a tea," Wela said, rushing into the kitchen.

I followed her and sipped on the tea my grandmother made me, my mind spinning. "They call you a witch, you know."

"I know." Wela laughed. "That's just as well. All I've ever done is help people."

"La Ciguapa is supposed to be a witch." I set down my tea. "And if she has backward feet, shouldn't you have backward feet?"

"I'm not a bad witch," she said. "She is. She steals men from good women."

"Why would she do that?"

"Because her soul is lost and stuck here. Some say she's waiting for the right one. The right soul will break the curse and set her free."

"I don't understand." I yawned.

"Go to bed. Don't you worry. You're safe." My grandmother helped me to my room and into bed. As my eyes fluttered shut and I drifted to sleep, I heard her praying over me, for my safety, for my peace. I smiled. That night, I dreamed of a wolf with yellow eyes. A wolf that followed me everywhere, lurking, waiting.

He was undressing me slowly, as if savoring every inch of skin he uncovered. I closed my eyes, relishing his fingers on me, the way his hands seemed to trace every sensitive part of my body, the way he seemed to know where I wanted to be touched. When I felt his mouth on my breasts, I stopped breathing, stopped thinking, stopped existing, my life suspended in a moment of time. He made his way down my body, his tongue finding every crevice, his teeth biting down on every surface, and his mouth following closely behind soothing the pain the bite marks left behind. It wasn't soft. It wasn't rushed. It just was and it was perfect. When he bit the insides of my thighs, my heart started beating hard against my chest, so hard I could barely breathe. His mouth found the spot begging for attention and he devoured it, devoured me, until I thought I just might cease to exist. The orgasm rushed over me quickly and when I felt him moving back up my body, I finally opened my eyes to see River staring back at me. River, with glowing yellow eyes that seemed to take in what was left of me with him.

A slamming door startled me awake. I sat up quickly, disoriented, heart beating quickly, liquid pooling between my legs, despite myself. It took me a second to remember where I was. The apartment above Dolly's bar. Dress shoes tapping against marble floors alerted me that someone was coming this way, but I stayed put, figuring it had to be Gustavo and that he'd knock before barging in. The knock never came, but the footsteps stopped on the other side of the door just before the knob turned and it was opened. I swallowed at the sight of River standing there. He was holding the hook of a garment bag over his shoulder in a way that made him look like he was modeling, not that he needed further help in that department. He looked every bit a model in the tuxedo he had on, with his dark hair perfectly brushed to the side.

"What are you doing here?" I managed.

"In my apartment?" His eyes glimmered.

"I thought you said you were sending Gustavo."

"I was, but then I thought, what if she backs out? What if

she needs some persuasion?" He cocked his head as he looked at me. "I like seeing you in my bed."

I swallowed. "I wasn't going to back out."

"Good." He pushed away from the doorframe, bringing the garment bag in his hand around and laying it flat on the bed. "I'll give you some privacy. No need to rush."

He glanced at the Rolex on his wrist. I only knew what it was because my father had the same exact one, a silver and gold band with a gold face. *Not obnoxious or overly expensive*, my father had said once. I nodded at River, keeping my eyes on the garment bag. I didn't trust myself to look at him again right now. When he left the room and shut the door behind him, I took a deep breath, feeling the air come back to my lungs once more. Further relaxation would be impossible, so I grabbed the garment bag and headed to the bathroom.

CHAPTER FOURTEEN

I COULDN'T WEAR A BRA, AND THE WAY THE FABRIC PLUNGED IN THE front and exposed my cleavage left little to the imagination. It fit beautifully, though, hugging me in all the right places while looking effortless, the way only silk fabric could. I smiled at my reflection. It took me thirty-five minutes to style my hair into loose waves and another thirty to apply my perfectly contoured makeup. The only thing missing was the red lipstick to match the dress I had on. I was afraid it might be too much, that I might look overdone if I applied it, though, so I was putting it off, wishing I knew what everyone else was wearing to the party, wishing I had more information—period. I'd tried texting Dee, but she hadn't responded. I knew her well enough to know she'd dress to the nines and with that in mind, I applied the lipstick.

The bedroom door opened behind me and I watched

as River walked inside and over to the threshold of the bathroom. His eyes met mine in the mirror, and I couldn't help the
way my heart reacted, thumping wildly with each loud tap his
dress shoes made against the marble floor as he neared me.
He stopped walking behind me and leaned against the doorframe, still staring, all nonchalant, as if he didn't look like a
walking wet dream.

"You're not wearing the necklace." His gaze raked over
me slowly, growing darker with every inch of me he took in.

"I . . . I couldn't put it on and then I didn't want to break
the clasp, so—" My explanation was cut short when he stepped
forward and picked up the necklace, bringing it around my
neck.

Our eyes met in the mirror once more as his fingertips
grazed my skin ever so softly. I shivered visibly, feeling his
touch spread through me like wildfire. He attached the clasp
of the necklace, securing it on me, and even though I felt the
weight of it on my neck, it was nothing in comparison to that
of his gaze on mine. I couldn't bring myself to look away.

"You're beautiful." His voice was soft, a mere whisper beside my ear. It wasn't like it was something I'd never heard,
but there was a reverence in his voice that made me shake
even as I thanked him for the compliment.

He took a giant step back and it was that breathing room
that pulled my gaze from his and made me finally look at myself again. A small gasp left my lips. The necklace glistened as
if the sun itself was around my neck.

"It suits you," he said. "The red, the diamonds."

"I'm not used to it." I let out a light laugh, glancing up at
him again.

"That doesn't mean you can't get used to it."

"I'm perfectly fine in my jeans. But I can see why some women like this." I turned to face him. "My mother loved getting all dressed up. Loves." I frowned, realizing that I didn't know anymore. I hadn't known for a while.

"We should head out." He offered me his hand and I was surprised at how easy it was for me to take it and keep my hand in his.

This was definitely not the way a sworn enemy should behave. No. Surely, I should be a little more resistant toward him, but then, what would the point of that be? He'd already chosen me as his company again today and as much as I didn't care for the townspeople talking about me or telling my grandmother all about this, I was less enthused to spend the night in jail. Besides, River Caliban was entirely too good-looking and magnetizing for me to not hold hands with. He locked the door behind us and led me downstairs, where Gustavo was waiting by the staircase. In the bar, there seemed to be triple the amount of people that there were last night. Everyone dressed in scandalous attire—bedazzled bras and thongs, the men in speedos and painted torsos, all of them wearing enormous masks that covered their faces and extended up to the ceiling. I let go of River's hand.

"What's the matter, afraid they'll think you like me?"

"Who says I like you?" I raised my chin defiantly, meeting his dark expression with my own.

"No one has to say you do." His eyes danced. "But we both know that doesn't mean it's not true."

"I don't." I swallowed, heart pounding, and walked forward, leaving him behind as I made my way to the door.

The crowd seemed to part for me, for us, all eyes staring, no one speaking a word. I wondered what they were thinking.

If they were tourists, they were probably wondering why the hell we were wearing such fancy clothes during Carnival. If they were locals, they were probably judging the hell out of me, probably thinking that they'd protested for me last night and here I was going willingly. It was that thought that made me keep my head held high as I walked outside. Yes, I was leaving with the rumored Devil again. Yes, I'd go to Dolos Island, to the Caliban Manor, but I'd do it my way. At least I hoped that was the bravado I was portraying because inside I was a ball of nerves.

Gustavo rushed ahead, but stopped and stood by the back doors when River held a hand up.

"I'll be driving Miss Guzman myself," he said. "It seems she wants to put on a show tonight, so I guess I'll play along."

Gustavo shot me a look of disdain. He obviously didn't like the way I was treating his boss and that was just as well. It wasn't like I'd caused a scene. I hadn't yelled. I hadn't stormed out. I'd just walked ahead of him and refused to hold his hand in public. How was that a scene? Every single thought that crossed my mind made me angrier than the last. River walked to the sports car parked in front of the Rolls Royce and held the passenger door open for me. I obliged, getting in the car and pulling on my seatbelt as I waited for him to get into the driver's seat. He started driving without saying a word and I realized he wasn't heading in the direction of Dolos Island.

"Where are we going?"

"Taking a drive." He glanced over at me. "Do you have somewhere to be?"

"I mean, shouldn't we be at the party?" I looked at the clock in the middle of the car. It was five-thirty and the party started at six according to Dee and Martín.

"Are you in a rush to get there?"

"Not particularly."

"Good."

He drove onto gravel and stopped when we reached the Devil's Peak, which made me laugh.

"What's so funny?" He put the car in park.

"The fact that you brought me here, of all places." I looked from the ocean just beyond us and to him. "You know people call you the Devil, right?"

"I never had the luxury of caring what people thought of me." He got out of the car and I followed, wobbling slightly. "This is my favorite place on your island."

He leaned against the hood of his car and I did the same. It wasn't that I wanted to stand close to him, but this was called the Devil's Peak for a reason. People died here all the time. Tourists lost their lives trying to take selfies with the ocean behind them. Locals lost their footing trying to scale down the rocks. Regardless of the reason or expertise, one thing was for certain and that was that I didn't want to venture too close to the edge and River's car was definitely not close enough. Besides, if he tried to throw me over, I'd pull him with me.

"What do you know about the curse?"

"This again?" I groaned, throwing my head back. "I don't believe in curses and I don't know much about it either way. I know everyone here thinks your family worships the Devil. Some say your father made a pact with him and that's the real reason that island you live on was torn from this one." I met his gaze. He seemed interested in what I was saying, curious even. "I know people don't make it out of Dolos. A lot of people have died in that ocean." I jutted my chin toward the water below us, the waves crashing hard against the rocks as I said it, as if confirming.

"What if I told you that most of that was real?"

"I'd say I still don't believe in curses."

"That's fair." He chuckled. My heart stopped when he did that. "Tell me about The Haunt."

"My website?" I blinked. "Have you been on it?"

"I have. I find it fascinating that there are that many people who love decaying things." He cocked his head, "Though, maybe I shouldn't find it that interesting. We are all decaying after all."

"I thought nothing ever dies?"

"It decays though." He cocked his head. "What I find more fascinating is that a woman from Pan Island, which is filled with fables and legends, would start a website like The Haunt and truly not believe in any of it."

"It's not that I don't believe in it per se." I pursed my lips, trying to figure out how to explain it. I hadn't in so long. "I think you can believe in ghosts and not believe in curses and vice versa."

"In The Haunt, you focus mostly on decaying houses, the ones that need restoration. You don't think homes with that much history are prone to ghosts?"

"Maybe." I met his gaze again. "You know, people say Dolos is filled with ghosts, lost souls that never made it back to wherever it was they came from. Do you believe that?"

"I do."

I raised an eyebrow. "That surprises me."

"Why?"

"Why would you live there if you truly felt it was haunted?"

"Who says I'm not the one they should be afraid of?"

My heart skipped as I watched his eyes darken. I swallowed, pushing down my trepidation. I needed to change the subject. Talking about haunts and ghosts on the verge of a cliff was definitely not my idea of fun, and that was saying a lot for someone who did what I did for a living.

"Do you have a cell phone?"

"What a question." The side of his mouth turned up as he pushed off the car and went back to the driver's seat.

"Do you have friends?" I followed and got in the passenger's seat, eyeing him as I put on my seatbelt.

"Of course, I do." He chuckled. "You'll meet some of them tonight."

"Did you go to college?"

"Did you?" He raised an eyebrow and I knew he knew the answer to that.

My lips pursed. "I couldn't afford that specific luxury."

"I beg to differ." He turned the car back on and we both reached for the air vent, our fingers crashing. I yanked my hand away quickly, ignoring the palpable electricity he elicited from me.

"How so?" I folded my hands on my lap.

"I think you could afford any luxury. You just choose the ones that give you instant gratification rather than the ones that may not, like a college degree."

"Well, considering the fact that most people I went to high school with ended up with a college degree and no job security upon graduation, I think I'm doing okay." I shrugged. "I have no student loans. They do."

"I can't argue there." His gaze flicked to mine briefly and then back to the road.

"Why'd you take me there?"

"To the Devil's Peak?"

I nodded.

"I don't get to go there often."

"Why not?" I watched the side of his face. "You have an apartment in town and everything. You're obviously over here often enough."

"I'm in a lot of places." He smiled, a small, secretive smile. "And yet, I'm not."

"What does that mean?"

"It's difficult to explain." He stopped in front of the black iron gates, and Gustavo was on the other side, unlocking and opening it.

"Why don't you have a mechanical gate like everyone else?"

"And throw away the—what did you call it—antiquated vibe this whole place has?" River laughed, the sound vibrating my pulse.

"Hilarious." I rolled my eyes, but couldn't keep myself from smiling.

I realized as we drove up the winding road and the gravel gave way to cobblestone and greenery, that the house was as well-lit as I'd ever imagined it could be, with torches outside, probably to keep the mosquitoes at bay, and grand lamps up the steps. It still looked every bit a dark manor, but something felt different about it. It was as though it was happy to have people in it. It was odd though, being that it was just a house, but it stuck.

As the doors opened before us, I reached out for River's arm. I didn't love being the center of attention, especially with this many people, and there were a lot. A lot more than yesterday. There must have been at least sixty people in attendance; it was a lot more than I'd anticipated, and every single one, man and woman, was staring. I began feeling self-conscious and grabbed onto River a little tighter.

"Relax. You're the belle of the ball." I could hear the smile in his voice even though I was too busy trying to find familiar faces in the crowd.

"Sir River Ambrose Caliban and his guest Miss Penelope Maria Guzman." The announcement came from a woman's voice, which I traced back to Fabiola, the woman I'd seen at the bar last night. She smiled at me, then at River, then at the crowd. Everyone clapped, which made the entire thing feel even more awkward. River let go of my arm to make a slight bow. I just stood there, unsure of what to do, so I smiled slightly, uncomfortably. River's hand reached for me, and this time instead of offering me his arm, he slid his fingers through mine and held my hand, squeezing slightly before he started to walk the room with me at his side.

"I'd pick Fabiola over Mayra any day," I said through the fake smile.

"I'm sure she'd be pleased to hear it." He introduced me to some of the attendees, some it was obvious he knew, but others, like the man we were shaking hands with currently, seemed to be taken aback by his presence altogether.

"Mr. Sir. Mr. Caliban." The man shook his hand. "Carson Emerson. I'm an old friend of your father's."

"It's a pleasure to meet you, Mr. Emerson." River smiled and turned to me. "This is my date, Penelope Guzman."

"Guzman?" Mr. Emerson's brows rose. "As in . . . that Guzman family? From Pan Island?"

"Yes, that family." I kept a tight smile and let go of River's hand.

"I'm sorry to hear about your father," he said, but he was looking at me like there was a lot he was leaving out.

"Thank you." I looked around. "I'm going to go find a drink."

"Call over one of the waiters," River said, waving someone over before I could. He let go of my hand and turned to a young man who tapped him on the shoulder.

"The man, the myth, the legend," the guy said with a chuckle. "I haven't seen you in a while, man."

"Always a pleasure, Alistair," River said, greeting him.

Mayra appeared in front of me with a tray in hand. She handed me a champagne flute. She wasn't glaring at me, but she also wasn't smiling. She was still wearing all black, but this time instead of a black long-sleeve shirt and skirt, it was a nice, long black dress.

"Thank you," I said, taking the flute.

"Of course." She grinned. "I do hope you're enjoying yourself."

"It's not my scene."

"I would think it was. Being the center of attention and all."

"Shows how little you know about me." I brought the flute to my lips and took a sip.

"Maybe I pegged all of you Guzmans to be the same. Your cousin lurks these grounds with his hollowed eyes and his empty heart." She shook her head. "All he does is complain. You have the entire world in the palm of your hands, yet you seek more; you leave the island you practically own and in search of what?" She shook her head again. "I will never understand it."

"Nor do I expect you to understand it." My eyes narrowed.

"You say my cousin lurks here, but that's wrong. Legend has it that the only lost souls that haunt the island are the ones who died here."

"Obviously." She shot me a look. "You're going to preach to me truths about my own birthplace?"

"My cousin didn't die here."

"Didn't he?" She raised an eyebrow. "Have you considered why you're here at all?"

"Because your boss chose me to be." I shot her a look.

"Right." She let out a laugh, and seemed truly humored by this. "Have you not questioned the accident at all? How it was, in fact, that seaplane would have gone down on a perfectly sunny, cloudless day?" She raised an eyebrow. "Unless . . ."

"Unless what?"

"Unless someone caused it."

"What are you saying?" My heart thumped louder, in my ears, in my chest.

"Exactly what you think I'm saying." Mayra raised an eyebrow, smiling as she walked away.

I looked at River, who was talking to his friend. He couldn't have caused the accident, could he? How? And my cousin? How would he have died here? I shook my head. Mayra was untrustworthy. I wasn't going to take her word for what actually happened with the accident. She'd wanted me gone from the moment I got here. After a moment, I walked over to River.

"Oh please, all of us are immigrants here. Our ancestors all arrived from someplace else." That was River, still speaking to his friend behind me.

"Some of our ancestors didn't have a choice in the matter," I said.

"Here we go." River shook his head. "So, now you're blaming me for something some of my ancestors had a hand in?" River raised an eyebrow.

"Not blaming. Simply pointing out facts."

"She's not wrong." The guy smiled, giving me a slow once-over. "What's your name, sweetheart?"

"Penelope and I'm not a sweetheart."

"She's not wrong. This one bites," River said, bringing his hand down to mine and threading his fingers through mine again.

His friend's brows rose. "Just when I think River Caliban can't do something that surprises me, he goes and gets himself a girlfriend."

"I am not his girlfriend." I tried taking my hand from River's, but he held on tighter. I glanced up at River and smiled. "You can try to hold on as tight as you want, but I'll still slip through your fingers."

"I have no doubt that you will, but I won't let that happen until I'm done with you." His mouth pulled into a slow, lazy grin that didn't reach his eyes. "And I'm not done with you yet."

CHAPTER FIFTEEN

THE DOORBELL RANG LOUDLY, AN EIGHT-NOTE CHIME THAT WAS familiar because most people I knew on Pan had the same one. We all turned our attention to the door just in time to see Dee, Martín, Jose, and a guy I didn't know walk through it. I felt myself breathe a little easier, and let go of River's hand again. This time, he let me. I beelined over to the front door and fell into Dee's arms when she opened hers the moment she saw me.

"Are you okay?" she asked quietly. "You look stunning."

"I'm fine." I pulled away and looked at her. She was wearing a black ballgown with a V-neck that plunged near her belly button. "You look amazing."

"Thank you." She smiled, eyeing my necklace. "What is this you're wearing?"

"River loaned it to me."

"Wow." She let out a sighed laugh. "So, is it safe to assume he's not so bad?"

"The verdict is still out."

"But you're safe?" She searched my eyes.

"I mean, if you think being in a gloomy house that's falling apart under the same roof as a jilted ex-lover who wants to kill you safe, sure."

"What?"

"She's not my ex-lover." That was River, who had snuck up behind us and made us both jump.

"She does want to kill me though," I said.

"Oh. Wow," Dee said, turning to look at River. "You look wow."

"Yeah, you look hot, but you already knew that," Jose added to River and then me, giving me a quick hug. "This is my date, Ricardo."

"Nice to meet you, Ricardo." I gave him a kiss on the cheek, and turned to Martín to kiss him on the cheek as well.

"You clean up nice as well."

"Especially for this gala," Martín said, looking around in awe. "It's just as creepy as I thought it would be." He looked at me. "Is it haunted?"

"I . . . don't know." I frowned. I'd seen something in the bathroom for sure, but not a person, not a ghost.

"Too bad," he said. "The Haunt would flip out if they knew you were in here."

"Maybe you should stay a little longer, Penelope, for the sake of The Haunt," River said, his eyes dancing.

"Yeah, no, I don't think so." I pursed my lips.

He let out a laugh. "I need to show you something. I do hope you all enjoy yourselves. Please grab drinks." He grabbed my hand again and escorted me away from my friends. I only had time to glance over my shoulder and see Dee's smile of approval as she nodded.

"Where are we going?" I asked as he led me down the corridor he wouldn't let me walk down just this morning. The pounding in my chest grew louder, harder as we walked.

"I want to introduce you to my parents."

"Oh." I swallowed. "They won't join the festivities?"

"Maybe later."

"Is your father feeling well enough to?"

"No, but he'll join anyway."

The hall was dimly lit with gas lamps, as the rest of the house was, but the lamps were close enough to the portraits that I could sort of make them out. Most of them were of groups of men, around tables signing papers, watching as one of them made a discourse, posing for a painter. One photograph in particular caught my attention. I stopped walking in front of it and let go of River's hand. The painting had tents and people everywhere, but front and center there were two men and two women. They were all smiling wide. My hand rose slowly to touch it, but I let it drop before it got there. It was my grandparents. I'd never met my grandfather, but I knew his face, and I knew this painting because the same one hung in my grandmother's house before she moved in with my parents. I looked at River, who was standing there watching me with his hands in his pockets. *Who are they*, I asked, but not aloud, I couldn't get my voice to work.

Nevertheless, he answered. "Your great-grandparents. And mine."

"Where are they?"

"On this very island."

"Dolos?"

"Dolos before the curse. Before it broke off."

"Why would this be hanging here?" I glanced up at him. "After everything."

"Maybe as a reminder of what once was."

"Why would you want to remember an old friendship, especially one that supposedly wronged you?"

"Why do we study history?"

"To learn from the past and not make the same mistakes all over again."

"But do we ever truly learn? Some would argue that your presence in this house would mean we don't."

"Mayra says my cousin haunts the Manor."

"Did she, now." River's lips set into a fine line.

"Is she telling the truth?"

"I thought you didn't believe in ghosts, in curses."

"Is she telling the truth?" I turned around and tilted my head to meet his gaze.

"Yes."

"Why didn't you tell me?" I asked.

He was standing far too close to me. So close that when he reached for me and wrapped an arm around my waist, I was powerless to stop him. So close that when he brought his face down, his nose touched mine and I stopped breathing entirely.

"What do you want to know, Penelope?" he murmured against me.

"Everything."

"Everything?" He pulled away ever so slightly, just enough to look into my eyes.

"Yes."

"Be careful what you wish for, little witch. These walls just may grant them to you."

"Maybe I want them to." I swallowed.

"What will you do when you learn that everything you thought you knew was a lie?"

"I . . . I don't know." I blinked, feeling myself drifting, as if in a dream. "What's a lie?"

"You'll just have to wait and see." River leaned in again and pressed his lips against mine, kissing me softly, so softly my knees buckled.

His hold around me tightened as he deepened the kiss, his tongue flowing into mine, taking, granting. He felt familiar, yet entirely too exciting to have ever kissed me before. I'd remember this kiss. I'd remember these lips and this tongue and these hands. It felt like my dream, just like my dream, but this was real. When he broke the kiss and pulled away, looking at me with a longing that nearly broke my heart, I knew it was real.

"River?" a female voice called out down the hall.

"We'll be right there." He straightened, bringing me with him, and took my hand in his as he led me down the hall.

We stopped in front of a woman and I had to take a second to gather my bearings. It was Sarah, the blonde beauty from the stories. She was wearing a beautiful floor-length dark pink dress that matched the flowers I'd seen on their lawn, and a matching fascinator on her head that made it look like she was either going to a tea party or the Kentucky Derby. She was stunning. I'd seen pictures of her around town, pictures on Missing signs that her husband had placed all over the island, even though he knew exactly where she was and who she was with. Her husband was long gone, but Sarah's signs remained, faded and ripped up, but no one dared take them down.

No one on the island dared touch anything that belonged to a dead person. It would be like calling death upon yourself, cursing yourself. Still, despite the fades and tears and washed-up signs, Sarah's face always looked beautiful, but seeing her in person was something else. She didn't look like she'd aged a day, but that was impossible. I thought of the tree, of the leaves. As if reading my thoughts, she smiled.

"It's so nice to meet you, Penelope."

"Likewise," I said. "You can call me Penny."

"Oh." She looked horrified, her perfect mouth turning downward. "Nonsense, love. Pennies are bad luck and my son would never pick up bad luck anywhere, would you, River?"

"No, ma'am." He smiled. I looked up at River, then back at Sarah. I knew she wasn't his birth mother, but I'd believe it if they said she was.

"Come. Meet our patriarch." She moved out of the way, still smiling. "Wilfred. River is here with his date to see you."

"Hello." Wilfred Caliban called out as we walked inside the sitting area of what I assumed was their bedroom.

The sitting area was large, with a fireplace, two loveseats, and two chairs around a coffee table. We stopped walking there and waited as the footsteps approached and stopped by the fireplace. Wilfred Caliban, like Sarah, looked to be forty years old at the most. I was no longer holding River's hand, but I reached for it now. He seemed surprised by this, glancing over at me quickly, but instead of saying anything, he ran his thumb over my hand. The closer Wilfred got, the more I suspected he wasn't ill at all. His dark skin, darker than mine and River's, was tight, glowing, and his hair was pitch black but cut very low to his scalp, as if a barber had just passed a machine over it.

"Father, this is Penelope Guzman."

"Oh." Wilfred Caliban stopped dead in his tracks and looked at his son, then stared at me. "You chose a Guzman?"

"Yes. Remember we talked about this."

"Ah, yes." Wilfred's brows pulled in and I could tell he was lying to placate his son. "Are you Maximo's girl?"

"Yes." I swallowed.

"My condolences," Wilfred said with a nod. He looked at Sarah, shaking his head. "The bastard beat me in everything, even in death."

"Wilfred," Sarah warned.

"Well, no use in not welcoming you. You're here after all, and under the care of my son. How perfectly fitting." Wilfred smiled. "You're a real beauty."

"Thanks." I looked down at my feet, accepting the compliment but also making it known I didn't want any more of them.

"We won't take more of your time. The guests are waiting," River said. "I just wanted to bring her to meet you."

"Thank you for that." Wilfred nodded at River. "Take your time coming back out to the party. Sarah and I will be introduced now." He walked away and joined Sarah before they walked out of the room together.

River stared at the licks of the fire in front of us. I let go of his hand and wrapped my arms around myself wondering what the hell that was and what the hell I'd gotten myself into. The good thing was he said I could leave with my friends tonight and I fully intended to take him up on that. After this little meeting and Mayra's words, the sooner I left, the better.

CHAPTER SIXTEEN

L EAVE THIS PLACE.

The voice was whispered in my ear. I looked around quickly, heart pounding, but the only person standing in the room was River and he was staring up at the painting above the mantle. It was an odd painting. Black and white, more blacks than whites, all swirling around the canvas. I thought I saw a face. Eyes staring at me. I looked around again. Like every other room in this godforsaken house, this one was dim as well, gas lamps flickering off in a distance, the licks of the fire in front of us not doing much other than making me feel suddenly sweaty.

Leave the voice said again.

"Did you hear that?" I shivered and walked closer to River.

"Hear what?" He looked down at me.

"Someone's in here with us."

"There's no one here." River made a show of looking around. "We should get back."

"So, Sarah raised you?" I chanced a glance at him from the corner of my eye as we walked out of the room.

"She did."

"What happened to your birth mom?"

"What happens to anyone when they're finished with this life?"

"She died?"

"In plain terms."

"Plain terms." I let out a laugh. "There are only plain terms, River. We're human. Humans are plain. We like yes or no answers and black and white issues. Anything beyond that, we struggle with."

"Is this a segue to calling my ancestors slave owners again?" He stuffed his hands in his pockets as we walked.

"No." My lips pursed. "Mine were no better. This island has a lot of deep, dark secrets we don't talk about and there's a reason for that. When secrets surface, we can no longer hide from our truth."

"I think we can finally agree on something," he said. "But for the record, my grandparents were married in secret because their love was forbidden and I like to think they were in love."

"You didn't strike me as the hopeless romantic type."

"What did I strike you as?" His eyes glittered in amusement.

"I don't know. I've never met anyone like you before."

"Hm." He looked toward the party we were nearing again and I wondered if he ever felt flattered by anything he heard anymore.

"Are the same people invited to the gala every year?"

"Not every year, but the ones who aren't invited back beg for an invite."

"Why?" I laughed. "The party is fine and all, but I haven't seen anything spectacular. No offense."

"That's because you haven't walked into any of the rooms." He quirked an eyebrow as we reached the edge of the hall, where the house opened up once more and the foyer was packed with people.

"You act like I'm going to experience some sort of magical thing in them." I turned to him, not ready to join the festivities just yet.

"In plain terms." He faced me as well. "You just might."

"In plain terms magic doesn't exist."

"According to that logic, this island doesn't exist. I don't exist. We don't exist." River smiled, but it was a smile that spoke of a million sad tales. He brought a hand to my face. "They're not fables, little witch."

"If they're not fables, why would you live here? How would you survive this house if it really is full of deceit?"

"Isn't every house deceitful in one way or another?"

"Not the way you're saying, not with magic and disappearing acts."

"Maybe you should go into one of the rooms and see for yourself." He raised an eyebrow.

"Maybe I will." I jutted my chin up.

I was always up for a dare, after all. I glanced at a woman walking out of one of the rooms. She'd been wearing a flapper-looking dress, but it was now just barely hanging on her. Her lipstick was running down her face and her updo was completely undone. She looked like she'd been having sex in the room. And when a man followed closely behind her, zipping up his trousers, I knew they definitely had been.

"Is this an orgy?" I looked at River again.

"Some people partake in orgies."

"Do you?" I swallowed. I didn't know why I asked, but I was curious.

"I have."

"Will you tonight?"

"Do you want to?"

"Do I want to participate in an orgy?" I blinked. "Absolutely not."

"Then I won't either." He chuckled. "You are my guest, after all."

"Which is exactly why I assume you have something planned for me. Mayra seems to have an idea as to why I'm here."

"Why do you think you're here?"

"I don't know." I bit my lip, still looking at him. He was impossible to look away from. "I can't help but think you want me, like *actually* want me, and I don't understand why."

"Come." He offered me his hand. I looked at it for a moment before taking it and letting him lead me back into the party.

The moment we stepped away from the hallway, music blasted us. It was jarring. I looked around quickly, looked behind us, looked forward. Had it been playing all along? It was lively, a *Cuban Son*, to be exact. I only knew it because back in the day, we used to island hop—a little bachata in Dominican Republic, a little salsa in Puerto Rico, and a little Son in Cuba. Hearing it reminded me of my parents and thinking of them made me sad again, grief rolling through me like a wave. I thought of Wela, who said this was a celebration of life and that my father dying this week was a great honor. Of course, she'd meant Carnival back on Pan. I highly doubted she'd approve of my being here in Dolos, in the Caliban Manor, of all places.

"River," a man with a British accent called out, walking toward us quickly. He was handsome, of Indian decent, with a full beard that covered most of his olive skin. He had wise brown eyes and I knew instantly he wanted to make some kind of sales pitch. "I've been looking for you. We still haven't discussed the yachts."

"Right." River gave a nod. "Dev, this is Penelope. Penelope, this is Dev, an associate of mine."

"Pleasure to meet you, Penelope." Dev took my hand and pulled me to him, kissing me on either cheek. When he pulled away he gave me a once-over. "I know I don't usually meddle in your personal life, but this one is a keeper, River."

"I completely agree with you for once." River's hand squeezed mine as he looked at me. I felt my heart skip one beat too many.

"Shall we talk business? It'll only take a moment," Dev said.

"I'm okay. I should go find my friends anyway," I said to River before looking over at Dev. "It was nice to meet you, Dev."

"Pleasure was all mine." He bowed slightly as I started to let go of River's hand and walk away.

River held on to my hand and pulled me back to him, making my chest crash against his. "Don't go into the white room."

"Why not? Is that where the orgies take place?" I smiled

at his scowl. "Maybe I'll change my mind and decide to partake in something illicit after all."

"Please don't go in there." The plea in his eyes was enough to make me yield any warning from him, so I simply nodded slowly.

"I won't."

He let go of my arm and turned his attention back to Dev as I walked away and spotted Dee and the rest of my friends.

"This party is amazing," she said, setting down her empty glass on a tray walking by.

"How much have you had to drink?"

"Not much."

"Alcohol hits differently here," Martín said.

"You said that about Pan." I eyed him, his glass, and then Jose and his date's.

"Yeah, well, it hits even harder here," Martín said, his words slurred. "You haven't uploaded any more pictures."

"I will soon. I have to edit them. I just took them this morning."

"I'm going back into the white room," Jose said, grabbing his date's hand.

"What's going on in that room?"

"Orgies," Dee said. "Gay, straight, whatever. It's interesting."

"You went in there?" My head whipped back to her.

"Just to watch. Martín doesn't want to take his clothes off here." She rolled her eyes.

"I'm wearing an Oscar de la Renta tux. One of a kind. I don't know who will see it and take it," he said. "The man is dead. It's not like he can make me another."

"That is actually totally understandable." I shrugged a shoulder.

"Who designed the dress you're wearing?" Dee asked, taking it in again. "It's so gorgeous and it looks like it was made for you."

"Carolina Herrera."

"Wow," Dee whispered, reaching out and touching the silk fabric. "Just wow."

"Yours is beautiful too." I smiled.

"Jenny Polanco." She winked. "We met Sarah Caliban earlier. She's wearing a Polanco piece as well."

"What'd you think?" I looked between Dee and Martín.

"Honestly? It's creepy after knowing the story," Martín said.

"They both look way too young for their age," Dee added. "Do you think they're vampires?"

"Vampires?" I laughed, then sobered up. I couldn't take any more magic talk. "Please tell me you're joking."

"Kind of. I mean, this house is so dark, only lit by gas lamps like we're in the 1920s, and they're so young-looking. How else do you explain it?"

"I can't." I shrugged.

"They're rich," Martín said. "Not rich like us, rich like *point eight percent of the world* rich. I think they do look their age, but they're devoid of the stress that others would have, so their skin is less wrinkled."

"Maybe," Dee said, though her expression was dubious. I agreed with her.

"During one of the tours of Pan Island," Martín started, "the guide said Wilfred's first wife died in the ocean trying to get back to Pan Island. They said that's the reason the ocean between Dolos Island and Pan is so angry."

"That's . . . " Dee shivered. "I don't want to think about drowning."

"Same. Let's talk about something else before my head explodes," I said. "Have you been to any of the other rooms, or is it just this dance area and the white room that are open?"

"I think I only saw that one," Dee said. "I just want to dance anyway. I don't want to explore more of the house. Who knows what lurks here." She shivered visibly.

"You can always go to the white room and check it out while we dance, Penny." Martín winked.

"I'm not sure I want to. I mean, I definitely don't want to join an orgy. This is a one-of-a-kind Carolina Herrera, after all." I winked back. Martín and Dee laughed.

"Well, we are going to dance," Dee announced, reaching for Martín's hand, then mine. "Join us."

"I'm fine right here. You two have fun." I smiled as she handed me a drink she'd grabbed from another waiter.

I walked closer to the band, watching as they played and sang as I sipped the drink in my hand. When I finished with it, I decided to explore. The thought of walking through the house alone spooked me, but there were too many people here for a scream to go unnoticed. At least that was what I told myself as I walked down the dark hall and found myself opening the first familiar door.

CHAPTER SEVENTEEN

I WAS ALMOST SURPRISED TO FIND THE STUDY EMPTY, BUT NOT surprised at the relief that washed over me. I lay my head against the door and closed my eyes as I gathered my breath. When I opened my eyes, I stared straight at the window across from me. The gift from the Pope. One of the Piuses, River had said. I wasn't up to date with my Pope knowledge, but I knew it had to be old. I walked over to it again. Maybe it was because it made me think of my grandmother, but I felt called by it. As I stood there, staring up at it, one of the candles beside me flickered. I turned my attention to it and froze when I saw a figure just beyond it.

"Who's there?" I turned to face the person, then looked at the desk beside me to see what I could make a grab for to use as a weapon if it came to that.

"Don't tell me you don't recognize your own cousin."

"Esteban?" My voice came out gasped, fear lodging into my throat. "B—but you're dead."

"Am I dead though?" He took a step forward, then another, but it was still too dark for me to see him and in my uneasiness, I found myself taking two steps away from him. "Have I been forgotten?"

"No, of course not." I swallowed, shaking my head. *This can't be real. This can't be real.* "You died. You disappeared. We assumed you died."

"I did."

"B-but that's impossible." My heart pounded harder in my ears. "How is this possible?"

"I'm tethered to this house, to this land, to whatever he wants me to be tethered to."

"Wh . . . who?" I stared at him, wishing I had the courage to walk forward and actually look at him, but I couldn't seem to move. My feet were too heavy to lift.

"Do you think I'm wicked?" he asked, ignoring my question.

I shook my head.

"If you just forgive me, I can move on. If you forgive me, he'll let me be in peace. I won't have to relive my death every day, the pain, the choking, the horror."

"F . . . f . . . forgive you for what?" My lower lip quivered.

"Look at me," he shouted. "Look at me!"

"I am. I'm looking at you."

"Look closely," he hissed. "I paid for what I did to you."

"I don't understand," I whispered, blinking away tears to keep them at bay.

Esteban had been my best cousin. Sure, he'd done questionable things, like take me to places I wasn't allowed, but he'd also gotten me out of trouble more times than I could count. Whatever it was he thought he did, well, of course, I'd forgive him. He stepped closer to the light and in it, I could see that his teeth were yellow, the front ones cracked, and his neck, oh God, his neck. It looked like someone had tied a rope around it and pulled mightily. His wrists too. I brought my hand up to my own neck and swallowed.

"Someone killed you?" I whispered, wiping the tears away. "Why? Who would do such a thing? Was it because you were stealing leaves for Tia Julia? To cure her of illness?"

"I was a thief," he said. "I took and I took. Just like my father did. Just like his father did. You need to forgive me." His voice was louder now, and it didn't sound like his at all. It sounded mean and demanding.

I took a step back, trying to figure out a way to get to the door quickly. *This isn't real.* It wasn't real but I didn't want to stay in here anyway. I crashed into the edge of the desk as I walked back. Esteban walked forward quickly, as if on skates, and stood directly in front of me.

"You need to forgive me." He reached out a hand and I half expected it to go straight through me.

He was admittedly a ghost, after all, wasn't he? His hand touched my shoulder. It was light and quick just as I moved away, but it was enough to render me motionless, breathless, unable to do anything at all. The door to the study opened and River walked inside.

"Leave." It was the only thing he said, his voice clear and loud, and the angry expression on his face as he looked in the direction of where Esteban was standing left no room for question.

When I turned my head to where my cousin had just

stood, he was gone. I stumbled backward, my hand on the edge of the desk the only thing keeping me from falling as I began hyperventilating. *What the fuck was that? What the hell just happened?*

"It's okay. You're okay." It was River, but he sounded like the man by the Devil's Chair.

The thought occurred to me seemingly out of nowhere, but when my head whipped in his direction, I knew I was right. Not for the first time since I got here, I wondered what I'd gotten myself into and whether or not it would be too late for me to leave. My eyes grew tired, heavy, and suddenly, just like that, I fell asleep.

CHAPTER EIGHTEEN

"**N**O ONE NEEDS TO KNOW ABOUT THIS," ESTEBAN SAID. "THEY won't believe you anyway."

I shook my head. I was scared, but I couldn't bring myself to say no, to tell him to stop. I was wearing a skirt, so when he climbed over me and put a hand over my mouth and another hand between my legs, the only thing I could do was scream into it, shut my eyes tightly, and pray it would be over soon.

It was.

It was over sooner than I'd anticipated. I couldn't bear to look at him. I looked out into the darkness instead, my gaze on the fog covering the streets, covering us. This was why Papi didn't want me out at night when Carnival was set to happen. Bad things happened after dark, but Esteban had promised him I'd be okay, that he'd look after me, so Papi let me come anyway. A sob escaped my throat.

"Oh, come on, that wasn't bad." Esteban nudged my foot with

his. "Someone had to do it and prepare you for the real thing. We don't have time for that now though."

I swallowed and tasted blood in my throat.

"I'm going to go get some leaves from that tree. It's just across the gates. I'll be right back." He loomed over me. "Stay here."

I nodded, biting my lip so hard I realized where the taste of blood was coming from. I listened as he left and then I cried. I cried until my face was full of snot and tears and my chest was heaving from it. When I was finished crying, I stood. Something wet trickled down my legs, and when I looked down, I realized I was bleeding. That made me cry again. Esteban was supposed to be my protector. Everyone said he was like an older brother to me since I didn't have one. He wasn't supposed to . . . he'd never done anything like that before. I started walking. He'd told me to wait, but I wouldn't. I couldn't. I was bleeding. I walked by the iron gates and saw that they were shut.

"Are you okay?"

I gasped and whirled to look behind me. There was a man, a figure, someone dressed in all black. I shook my head and swallowed. My lower lip started to shake and then I started to cry. I was crying so hard that I didn't know how I ended up sitting in the Devil's Chair again. I'd just sat there earlier, when my friends dared me to, but that was before they left.

"Make a wish," the man said.

"I already did." I sniffled, wiping my nose with the back of my hand. "I wished to be rich."

"You already are."

"No, my parents are rich. I wish to be rich myself."

"What else do you wish?"

I bit my lip. I thought of Esteban, what he'd done. How he'd never own up to it. How things would go even if I did tell my parents *about it. They'd shake their heads and tell me I was crazy, that I was making it up, but I knew. I knew.* An awful sob raked through me, making my shoulders shake. *I wanted Esteban to suffer, the way he'd made me suffer. I wished I could leave. I wished I could leave so that I'd never have to see him again. That was what I wished.* As I walked home, I felt something watching me from the darkness of the forest beside me. When I glanced over, I saw two golden eyes staring at me. When I blinked, I was standing in front of my house. I looked around quickly. How had . . . had I walked here? I ran up the driveway, clutching my hands into fists.

"Where did you get that?" My father opened the door before I got a chance to.

"I . . . " I looked around, feeling lost.

"Where's Esteban?" Papi asked.

"I don't know."

"Come inside." My father moved out of the way and looked outside briefly before turning to me and taking the camera from my hand. "You need to cover the lens, Penelope. How many times do I have to tell you? These are expensive." He sighed heavily and then looked at the screen. "How did you take this?"

"Take what?"

Papi left the room suddenly.

"Oh my God, Penelope. What happened?" Mami walked in and rushed over to me.

"I don't know." I shook my head and started to cry again. Mami held my head to her shoulder and shushed me gently.

"She went to Caliban Manor." My father stormed back into the room, screaming.

"Don't be ridiculous, Maximo. How would she have gotten there?"

"I didn't."

"She's lying." That was my father. "She has a picture of the Manor."

"I'm not lying. I don't know how that picture got there."

"Penelope." Wela gasped. "I told you to be careful. I told you to stay by Esteban."

"Esteban touched me. He . . . he violated me," I shouted, then started to cry again, harder now that I'd said the words aloud.

"He what?" My father roared.

"What do you mean, Penny?" Mami asked quietly. "Surely, your cousin wouldn't . . . "

"You don't even know what you're saying?" Papi asked.

"Did he put his . . . you know . . . " Mami asked, tears welling her eyes.

I shook my head. He hadn't put his penis inside me. Only his hand. Forcefully. Painfully.

"Oh, thank God," Mami said.

"She could be lying." My father shook his head. "He's a good kid. He wouldn't—"

"That's not true," I shouted, standing. "I am not lying. He hurt me."

"With the company you keep I find it hard to believe you'd even be a virgin," Papi said.

My grandmother did the sign of the cross on herself.

"Stop it this instant, Maximo." My mother stood. "Go look for Esteban."

"I will not question Esteban about this. His mother is dying. His father just died. Do you think this is fair to him?" Papi asked, then looked at me. "You need to get out of my house. You betrayed us. You betrayed our family when you decided to go to the Caliban Manor."

"I didn't go. I didn't."

"Leave my house. Now." It wasn't a request.

I ran to my room and packed a bag. Mami sobbed. Wela picked up the leaves and cried quietly in the kitchen. When I walked back out of my room with my bag in my hand, Wela was the only one waiting for me. She had a cup and my camera in one hand and money in the other.

"Drink this," she cooed, kissing my forehead. *"Drink this. Everything will be fine."*

And so I did.

CHAPTER NINETEEN

EVERYTHING WAS ROCKING. THE ROOM WAS SWAYING. I SAT UP and screamed.

"Hey." River's voice was beside me.

I felt like I was going to start hyperventilating again, but he put a hand on my shoulder and I instantly felt calm. I was scared to look at him. I was scared to look anywhere, but my eyes were on the sitting area in his bedroom, and so I knew I'd been lying in his bed again. Had it all been a dream? I swallowed. No. It hadn't. Even the worst nightmares aren't as awful as reality. I buried my face in my hands.

"Is the party still going? Are my friends still here?"

"Yes."

"What happened to me?" I whispered.

"You remembered."

"Was that . . . were you the one . . . " I swallowed. "Did you kill him?"

"Yes."

I pulled back. *Yes.* He didn't even bother looking sorry about it either. I swallowed past the knot in my throat and took a deep breath. "Did you kill my father?"

"What?"

"Did you kill my father?" It was harder to get the words out the second time, with the knot in my throat and words that tasted bitter on my tongue.

"Yes." His mouth formed a flat line. "Indirectly."

"What does that mean?" I managed, my voice barely a whisper. "What does *indirectly* even mean?"

"It means he died because of an accident I caused, but I did not mean to kill him."

"God." I brought a hand up, brushing against the diamonds on my neck before covering my mouth to stop the sob that wanted to rip out of me.

"I would have stopped at nothing to get you here."

"Why? Why do you need me here?" I let out a choked laugh, tears blurring my vision. "God. That would almost sound romantic if it wasn't so deceitful."

"Isn't that all romance is? Deceit wrapped up in a pretty package."

"Real love isn't deceitful." I blinked, wiping under my eyes with the tips of my fingers.

"What do you know about real love, little witch?"

"Don't call me that." This time when I spoke, the anger registered in my voice. "I . . . I can't breathe with you in front of me right now."

River stood up and walked a couple of steps away from the bed.

"You killed my cousin because of me." I wiped my face

and finally looked at River. "I sat in that chair and made that wish and then he died."

"You didn't wish for him to die."

"It's all the same, isn't it? His ghost is still here. In this house."

He shook his head. "His ghost is your memory. Your memory has kept him alive, and so, he appeared for you in his true form. That's what happens during Carnival."

"You choked him to death," I whispered, hating that it hurt so much to speak the words aloud. Hating that I was upset by any of it even after what he did to me.

"I did worse than just choke him," he said. "You asked him if I knew him, and I did. When he worked here, I even went as far as befriending him." He shook his head. "But how does one un-see what he did to you?"

"You saw it happen?"

"Not when he did what he did. I would have killed him then. I put two and two together when I saw you crying and then when you sat in the chair I saw it . . . "

I searched his eyes. "It's true what they say then."

"What do they say?" His mouth turned up slightly.

"That you're the Devil."

"Plain terms."

I clasped my hands together and brought them to my chest.

"What are you going to do, little witch? Start praying?" He raised an eyebrow. "Don't you think it's a little late for that?"

"I want to go home with my friends."

"Your friends are in no state to go home." He stood and walked to the fireplace, looking at the ships in the painting. "Besides, the tide's up for the night."

"I thought the tide stayed low this week. I thought that was the point of the party."

"I'm not the keeper of the ocean. Are you?" He glanced over his shoulder at me. My heart dipped. My grandmother did always say the Devil was charming and seductive. She wasn't lying.

"Why me?" I'd asked the question a million times and never got a clear answer.

"I'll tell you." He turned to face me. "If you stay through the week."

"Through the week?" My eyes widened. "That's . . . two more nights."

"That's my condition. Two nights and you take the leaves when you go."

"How do you know about . . . " I let my question trail off. Of course, he knew about the leaves. He seemed to know everything about me. It was an unfair advantage, but then, it had been from the beginning. I met his gaze and nodded once. "I'll stay through the week."

His smile was blinding.

Sinful.

Promising.

Wicked.

CHAPTER TWENTY

I HAD NO DESIRE TO SEE ANY GHOSTS, SO I DECIDED TO STAY INSIDE River's bedroom. He stayed with. He only let me out of his sight so that I could shower and change, and he did the same before settling in the sitting area to read a book. I kept replaying the memory over and over in my head. Esteban on top of me, touching me forcefully. I shivered. I couldn't believe I'd forgotten it.

"The tea," I said. River looked up at me. "The tea made me forget."

"The leaves can do that."

"My grandmother used those leaves for a lot of things. To cure people, to help them, and to make me forget." I shook my head. "Why do I remember everything else? I didn't even remember he disappeared that same night."

"We believe what we want to believe." River went back to his book.

"Are you human?" I tried to keep my voice level, but the question was quiet. Maybe I didn't want to know.

"I am." The edge of his mouth lifted.

"But are you not—"

"The Devil?" He glanced at me over the book. "I don't know. Are you not a witch?"

"I'm not."

"You come from a long family of witches. Many of whom were burned at the stake."

"For having strong opinions about things."

"For practicing witchcraft, Penelope. Even you can't kid yourself into thinking they weren't. Your grandmother is one of the island's most sought-out healers." He raised an eyebrow.

"Healer doesn't mean witch."

"Outcast doesn't mean Devil."

I leaned back against the headboard and stared at him. His gaze flicked from me back to his book, which was apparently more interesting. I crossed my arms. I was fully intending to say something snappy, but my mind drifted back to the memory.

"My father didn't believe me," I said after a long moment. River lowered the book and looked at me, but didn't say anything. He just waited. "He didn't believe me about my cousin when I told him. He said he wouldn't bother Esteban because of everything he'd been through and then kicked me to the curb like I was Thursday's trash." I brought my knees up to my chest and hugged myself.

"I'm so angry. And sad. But mostly, angry. For years I wanted my father to call me, to forgive me for the picture I didn't remember taking. To be proud of me for everything

I'd accomplished and . . . " I shook my head and swallowed again. "For what? He didn't even side with his own daughter."

"He didn't know how."

I glanced up and met River's gaze again. The room was dark, but I could swear I saw the compassion in his eyes.

"Sometimes men don't know how to deal with the mistakes of another, so they ignore them instead." He shut his book and set it down, sitting back in the daybed and stretching his long legs out. "We make excuses for ourselves in hopes for our salvation. We ignore others' wrongdoings so that we don't have to look too closely at our own. It's the way we survive."

"That doesn't make what he did okay."

"It doesn't."

"It doesn't make what you did okay."

"I've learned to live with my sins, little witch. I don't need your judgment, or your penance."

"I'm not a witch." I felt myself scowl.

River looked like he wanted to smile, but didn't.

I yawned loudly. "I can't believe I'd actually go to sleep after all of that."

"Sleep." He stood up and walked over to one of the gas lamps, switching it off. He was wearing khaki pants and a white button-down and didn't look ready for bed at all.

"Will you . . . " I bit my lip. "Are you going to stay?"

"Do you want me to?" He paused by the fireplace. "After everything?"

I nodded. I didn't know why. It didn't make sense. I should be angry with him. I should never want to see his face again. And yet . . . I sighed. River turned around and clicked another lamp off before walking over to the bed and sliding under the covers. I lowered my legs and scooted farther down in bed until my head was on the pillow.

"I had a dream about you." I licked my lips.

"A good dream?"

"I'm not sure."

"Hm."

I turned in bed, facing him, even though now the room was pitch black and there was no chance of me seeing him at all. "Do you dream?"

"Everyone dreams."

"Do you have good dreams?"

"Only when you're in them." I could hear the smile in his voice when he said it, so I knew he was making a joke. My face went hot anyway. God. If he only knew the dream he'd starred in. "Good night, little witch. I hope you dream about me again tonight."

I opened my eyes to the sound of murmuring voices nearby and turned to see that River was no longer beside me. When I sat up, I followed the sound of the voices to the door, which was slightly parted. River wasn't there though, but I could make out a dog standing there. A large dog. A wolf. As if sensing me, the wolf looked over at me, yellow eyes glowing in the darkness, and looked away once more. The person on the other side of the door said something else, but this time no one answered. I held the comforter higher on my chest. For some reason, the wolf didn't elicit fear in me the way you'd think an animal known to be vicious would. I wanted to stay up, wanted to keep my eyes open, but instead, I lay back down and closed them.

When I woke a second time, I sat up quickly, looking around. There were two lamps on now and no River in bed again, but I could hear the faint sound of the shower so I assumed he was in there. The bedroom door opened suddenly, and I gripped the comforter tightly. If I saw Esteban again I wasn't sure what I'd do. Run? Scream? What could I do to a ghost that could touch me? It was Mayra.

"Breakfast is served."

"Oh. Okay." I felt myself frown. "Aren't you supposed to knock?"

"I never knock on Master Caliban's door." She smiled a small, secretive smile that spoke volumes. He'd said they weren't lovers. Had he lied? Did it matter? I was quick to gather my bearings. I'd had a hell of a night. If I could face a ghost from my past, surely I could flick off a little gnat like Mayra.

"Well, please knock next time. After all, I am staying here as well, and I don't wear clothes to bed." I smiled the same secretive smile right back. She glared and shut the door with a loud thump.

The bathroom door opened. I hadn't even heard the water turn off, but River was standing there bare chested, wearing khaki pants as he towel dried his hair.

"That was Mayra. She wanted you to know breakfast is ready." I stood from the bed and walked over to the bathroom, feeling inexplicable anger rise with each step I took. I brushed past him and walked into the bathroom, ignoring the pull, ignoring the sudden, insane urge to claim him as mine. Instead, I kept my voice steady. "I need the bathroom now."

"She's not my lover." He dropped his hand, letting the towel in his hand hang.

"It doesn't matter."

"It does to you."

"Why would it matter to me?" I scowled, crossing my arms and glancing away, but my eyes got caught on our reflections in the mirror and on his golden flesh and ripped body.

"That's a question you need to ask yourself."

"No, I don't." I looked away from the mirror and up at his face. "What I need to do is get out of here."

"You agreed to stay the week."

"I know, and I will. That doesn't mean I want to."

He set his mouth into a thin line and nodded once before walking away from me. When he was gone, I shut the bathroom door and went about my business. I'd dragged the trunk of clothing in here yesterday and was grateful that it was still here. Today, I dressed in a dark green shift dress and black heels, hoping it would serve as the pick me up I needed to get through this. Two more days. I brushed out my hair from the braid I'd slept in and let it cascade over my shoulders. When I finished, I walked back into the bedroom, where I found River sitting on the daybed, reading the same book he was reading yesterday. He was wearing khaki pants, black loafers, and a white button-down shirt. He looked all the bit prep school graduate, the type that had a sailboat and an expensive vacation home somewhere along a coast. I couldn't imagine that would be the case for River though.

"You done staring?" he asked, not looking up from his book.

"Yes." I glanced toward the door. There was no use in denying that it was what I'd been doing.

"Good. Let's go have some breakfast." He shut the book with a loud thump and set it down.

"You're not even going to mark your page?" I glanced at the book and back at him when he stood. Even with the three-inch heels I wore, he loomed over me. "Won't you lose your place?"

"It won't matter. I've read it before." He started walking toward the door. I followed quickly, my heels clicking loudly against the marble.

"That huge book?" My eyes widened. "Why are you reading it again?"

"Why does anyone reread a book or rewatch a movie?" He looked over at me as we headed down the stairs. "It brings a sense of comfort."

"I don't read much."

"That's a pity."

"Why's it a pity?" I let out a laugh.

"I pity those who can't get lost in fictional worlds."

"Oh. I mean, I read magazines and message boards on the internet about old houses and photography, but I don't read many books."

"Like I said, pity."

When we reached the first floor, I was surprised to see everything looked immaculate, as if there had been no party at all.

"Where'd everyone go?" I asked as we walked to the dining room.

"Home."

"I thought you said they couldn't get out of here." I felt myself frown as I sat in the same chair I'd sat in yesterday. River took a seat across from me.

"The tide lowered and they were able to after all."

"Hm." My frown deepened. The food was already laid out for us and we dug in right away. Well, I did. River let me serve my plate first. I sipped on my coffee and looked up at him. "I saw you last night. You were a wolf."

"A wolf?" He raised an eyebrow. "A protector. That's what your kind would say about that dream."

"My kind?" I let out a laugh. "You mean humans?"

"Sure."

His answer gave me pause. He'd already told me he was human, but the way he said *sure* like that, so flippantly, filled me with turmoil. Even more so because I realized that despite myself, I wanted to believe in someone, maybe even dream a little like one of the characters in the fictional stories he liked to read. It didn't make any sense, especially since by my own account I was dying to leave this place, but still. Far be it from crazy for me to be attracted to someone who didn't even end up being part of the human race. Maybe he was lying and was really a ghost, like Esteban. I met his gaze. He was watching me closely. Waiting.

"Are you human?" I asked, my voice a near whisper.

"Back to this?" He chuckled. "I'm whatever you need me to be."

"What does that mean?"

"If you want me to be a wolf, I'll be a wolf. If you want me to be your lover, I'll be your lover." His gaze darkened. "But yes, I am human. I'm not a ghost or some creature of the night if that's what you're worried about."

"I'm not worried about it." I cleared my throat, still trying to get over the lovers bit. "Why is it always so dark in here? Doesn't it drive you mad?"

"Why would it drive me mad? It's all I've ever known."

"You never answered my question the other day. Did you go to university? Or school in general?" I asked, correcting myself quickly. Maybe he'd been homeschooled.

"I did."

"Up to what grade?"

"Year four of medical school." His mouth curved. He was so amused by my questions and so damn sexy when he looked that way. I wasn't sure which of the two was more maddening.

"Medical school?" I raised an eyebrow. "I take it you didn't finish?"

"I didn't."

"But year four? You were so close to finishing. What happened?"

"Life." He sighed heavily.

"Hm. Where'd you attend undergrad?"

"Cambridge."

My brows rose. "And medical school?"

"Cambridge."

My jaw dropped momentarily. "Why are you here?"

"This is my home." He chuckled deeply. "Where else would I be?"

"This is your parents' home. You could easily get your own or finish your studies. Why didn't you finish?"

"My father needs me here right now and he needed someone to take charge of his investments."

"So medical school was set aside."

He nodded. That was commendable. It was the right thing to do. It was what my father would have wanted me to do had things gone differently between us. Then again, hindsight was twenty-twenty. It was probably something he wanted Esteban to do. Thinking about my father and Esteban made my stomach roll. I was no longer hungry.

"So my friends left without me." I glanced toward the ballroom, where everyone had been drinking and dancing last night.

"They'll be back tonight. It is a weeklong event, after all." He set his napkin down beside his plate. "I expect you'll want to join the festivities again?"

"I'm not sure I do." I pursed my lips. "I want to see my friends, but I don't think I want a repeat of last night."

"That's fair."

"And I don't want to dress to the nines again."

"You look beautiful regardless of what you wear."

I bit my lip and glanced away in hopes of hiding my blush. I needed to gather my bearings if I was going to stick around two more days. The last thing I needed was to hand my heart over to the Devil over some stupid leaves.

CHAPTER TWENTY-ONE

RIVER WENT TO THE STUDY TO TAKE SOME PHONE CALLS, BUT I couldn't bring myself to walk anywhere near it even after he told me that ghosts didn't cling to one specific room. I started heading back to the bedroom, but as I neared the stairs, I spotted Sarah walking out of the hallway.

"Well, hello, dear." She smiled brightly. "Are you busy?"

"No, I was just going back upstairs."

"Walk with me."

"Sure." I followed her to the back of the house. "I didn't see you at the party last night."

"Oh. I heard you had a bit of a scare." She looked over at me. It was so strange to see her up close like this after a lifetime of seeing faded pictures.

"I saw a ghost."

"A nice one or a bad one?"

"A familiar one."

"Those are the worst kind, aren't they?" Her nose scrunched up. "Sometimes it's best to do what they ask and let go of the past."

"Are you speaking from experience?"

"I am." She pulled open the door that led to the backyard and let me walk through first. The fog was heavier than it was yesterday, swirling all around us like a snake. "I don't think there will be a party after all tonight," she mused, looking around. "The conditions aren't ideal for travel."

"Do you ever leave this island?"

"Of course, I do." She smiled. "I've spent a lot of time in France. In Spain. In Lisbon. I feel happiest there."

"Why not move then?"

"My husband needs me." She smiled softly. "You asked if I speak from experience in regards to the ghosts." She stopped walking when we reached a tree. *The tree.* She began cutting leaves and putting them in a small wicker basket that was sitting beneath it. As she cut them, she looked at me. "My ex-husband haunted me in the beginning."

"In the beginning?" I frowned. "But he wasn't dead."

"Not physically, no, and yet, he haunted me just the same."

"How? Why?"

"I suspect he was clinging on to hope that I'd come back." She stopped clipping, folded the scissors, and put them away in the basket, sitting down underneath the tree and patting the spot beside her. I walked closer and sat down, folding my legs to the side. The grass was surprisingly dry.

"So he haunted you because he wanted you to go back to him," I said. "Do you think maybe it was your own guilt for leaving that haunted you?"

"No. Not really. I was horrified when Wilfred chose me.

I mean, I was already the talk of the town. I'd been married five years and had no children, and when that night came and Wilfred announced it was me he wanted, I . . . it was shocking to everyone."

"I bet. Men usually don't pick married women."

"Not for lack of wanting them or because of decency." She shot me a look. "I knew many women having affairs, but they'd never do anything to display it openly." She glanced back at the wicker basket on her lap. "My marriage was awful. My husband ridiculed me for not being able to get pregnant and we'd just had a huge fight about my worth and how little I was contributing, so when Wilfred called my name, despite reason, despite knowing how awful it would make me look, I was glad."

"It sounds like he saved you in a way."

"In many ways." She smiled. "And I saved him in many ways as well. River was in boarding school at the time. They'd just lost Rosie, River's birth mother." She looked at me. "The house shook when I got here. Visibly shook, as if grieving. I know the island is dark and can be a little spooky, but the house isn't the problem, it's the curse that looms over it."

"The curse set on it by my family."

"I've been told you don't believe in curses, but if you were to see a picture of the house before the curse and after you'd be forced to question that notion."

"Is there a way to get rid of it?"

She smiled sadly. "Some of the staff thinks that when my husband dies, the curse will lift. They could be right. There's no telling. You know what they say about the island though."

"It takes one and gives another back," I whispered.

Sarah nodded slowly, sadly, and I couldn't help but wonder if there was any other way, one that didn't require death.

CHAPTER TWENTY-TWO

RIVER

H E THOUGHT THERE MUST BE ANOTHER WAY. IT HAD TAKEN SIX years to get her back on Pan Island and a lifetime to get her on Dolos Island, and yet he wanted to look for another way. Any way that would spare both of their lives, but it seemed impossible. Maybe it was a doomed plan from the beginning. Maybe he should do what he was supposed to and take her to the cave, to the part of the island where, according to legend, according to the man in black, he could reverse all of this. He could restore everything back as it once was. He hadn't expected to enjoy her company as much as he did. He hadn't expected to enjoy laughter. Or light. Or any of the things he often read about but hadn't truly experienced in this way. He hadn't expected her to be the way she was, and so, he had to look for another way.

CHAPTER TWENTY-THREE

PENELOPE

IT WAS DARK AND DREARY, WHICH WASN'T A SURPRISE, BUT IT WAS also raining hard outside, and that hadn't happened since I'd arrived. I sighed, stepping away from the window and going back to the dinner table. River, Sarah, and I had finished having dinner, and she excused herself to go back to her room, leaving him and me here. We'd dressed for the party—him in a tuxedo, me in a floor-length silver and ivory gown. I'd said I didn't want to dress up, but when I saw it, I couldn't not wear it. It was similar to last night's in that it was also simple, also made of fine silk, and also didn't allow me to wear a bra.

"I want to show you something." River stood from his seat and held his hand out to me.

I took it and followed him out of the dining room. He

walked down the other hall, the one that led outside, but instead of going to the backyard door, he opened the door to the left. He let me walk inside first, following closely behind and shutting the door. It was dark. Pitch black, not even a gas lamp to light the way.

"River?" I whispered.

"One second." I heard him fussing with something, but I didn't know what, until the light illuminated. He held a lantern between us. "You need to follow closely behind me."

"Where are we going?" I asked, then paused when I heard a drip, then another. "What is that sound?"

The room was empty as far as I could tell. River walked and I followed and when we reached a rope hanging from the ceiling, he lifted his hand and pulled it down, bringing a staircase with him. He placed the lamp on the step in front of his face and looked at me.

"You'll have to trust me."

I stared at him. I didn't trust anyone. Especially not after yesterday.

"You'll have to at least trust me to ensure your safety." He searched my eyes. "What I want to show you is up there. You'll have to take your heels off, unless you trust yourself in them."

I reached down and slid off my shoes, carrying them by the heel in my right hand. "Now what?"

"Now you climb." He took a step back.

I swallowed and did as I was told. I was too curious not to and if the party wasn't happening that meant I wouldn't be seeing my friends tonight or leaving anyway. When I reached the top, I looked down and saw him climbing up behind me. Once we were both up, he pulled the stairs up and folded them flat. We were inside another dark room. The attic, I guessed. I'd never been inside of an attic before.

"Stay put," he said.

I did.

He walked somewhere and suddenly there was light. I gasped. Small tealights were hanging everywhere in the room. Not the kind of lights the rest of the house had, lit by candles and gas. These were real, electric lights. I didn't know why, but knowing that even this small part of the house was lit with electricity gave me hope. Not that I needed hope. I'd be leaving soon. I wouldn't get stuck here the way Sarah had. I walked forward. A large, wide window covered the longest wall, and even though it was dark out, I knew the moon was out there somewhere. There was a mattress beside the window and a fluffy white comforter that looked like the one on his bed.

"What is this place?" I turned to face him, the heels still dangling from my hand.

"It's my piece of the house." He was standing there, watching me as I took it in. Waiting for me to say something, as if my opinion mattered.

"It's lovely," I said finally, smiling when I looked back at him, and then, he smiled. "You have a beautiful smile, you know?"

"Do I?" He smiled wider. I forced myself to turn away from him.

"Why are you showing this to me?" I walked up to the window, surprised I didn't have to hunch over in order to stand there.

It was pretty tall considering. River walked up behind me, setting a hand over my hip. I tried to fight the electricity his touch passed through me, but it was no use. Instead of pulling away, I melted into him, my exposed back against the buttons of his button-down. I closed my eyes momentarily, just enjoying this moment, as if we were two lovers who'd known each other for years, who shared common interests, and hadn't been taught not to trust each other. Up here, none of that mattered.

"None of that matters anywhere." River's voice in my head had my eyes snapping open.

There was nowhere for me to pull away, but he must have sensed I needed space, because he let go and took a step back before I turned to face him.

"You . . ." I searched his face. "Can you read my mind?"

"Sometimes."

"You said you were human."

"I am human." He tilted his head, his voice lowering slightly. "And I feel like we're running out of time."

"Out of time for what?"

"Everything." He sighed heavily. "I want you to know me before you leave."

"What do you want from me?" My heels fell out of my hands, tumbling onto the wooden floor beneath us.

"I want everything and nothing at all."

"What does that mean?"

"I want you. It's that simple. I want you."

"Why?" I took a step back. "Why do you want me?"

"How could I not?" He let out a laugh.

"You don't even know me. You say you want me to know you, but you don't even know me."

"I do."

"You don't." I frowned.

He moved closer. I didn't move; despite my wild heart, despite my raging pulse, I stood still. I let him close the distance between us, let him caress the side of my face with his palm, and shut my eyes to relish his touch. My lips parted when his thumb grazed my lower lip. I opened my eyes then, looked into his.

"We're made of the same essence, little witch."

"Why do you call me that?" I whispered.

"People call my family witches. They want to cast stones at us, burn our land." His mouth pulled up slightly. "But you're the one who's bewitched me. From the moment I met you all those years ago, I haven't stopped seeing you, fantasizing about you."

"Why?" I whispered.

"I don't know. Some things are inexplicable." He dropped his hand from my face and looked over my shoulder. I traced his line of sight and saw that the skies were clear.

"How does that happen?" I looked at him. His gaze found mine once more.

"Sometimes everything lines up and the fog just lifts."

I nodded slowly. I felt those words deep inside me, as if he'd reached in and planted them there, and when he leaned in and kissed me, I molded my lips to his, my tongue to his movements, let him breathe into my lungs. His hands were slow, soft, as he undressed me, his mouth following every place his hands touched. His tongue was hot against my skin, on my collarbone, over my chest, on my breast. I gasped when his tongue flicked my nipple, my hands fighting to take off his jacket. He pulled back from me and undressed, shrugging the jacket off first, ripping off the tie, then working on each button of his button-down and pants. My dress met the same fate as my shoes and the only thing left was the thin thong I wore. I left it on just as he'd left on his black boxer briefs.

"You look like an underwear model."

"I'd say the same about you, but you're not wearing much." He smiled. God. That smile.

"You should be a sin."

"Maybe I am." He took a step forward, bringing both hands to either side of my face. "Would you pray against me?"

I shook my head. "I don't pray much."

"Hm. A sinner then."

"Maybe." I tilted my chin a little higher, asking, begging, and then, I froze.

"What's wrong?"

"I've never done this before," I whispered, my lower lip quaking slightly. "Not like this."

"Like what?" He kissed my forehead, then each eyelid as I shut my eyes.

"Granting permission," I whispered. I felt uneasy suddenly, but the expression on his face was devastation, comprehension, and compassion.

"You told me, remember? When you sat down in that chair," he said. "I believed you. I believed every word you told me. I fought for you."

A sob got trapped in my throat. I swallowed and nodded, tears stinging my eyes and trickling down my face. He had believed me and he'd been the one to take vengeance in my name. Not my father. Not my mother. Not my grandmother, but a stranger. A stranger I'd been told to stay away from, to be deathly afraid of. I wrapped my arms around River's neck and pulled his face to mine, taking a kiss, desperate for him, desperate to forget, to remember, to feel, to just *be*. He kissed me with the same ardor and lay me on the bed as he explored my body with his mouth. I explored his with my hands, each rigid muscle, and when I wrapped my arms around his back, I felt a scar, then another, and another. I gasped, but it wasn't at the feel of his imperfections, it was because he began moving down my body, settling his head between my legs. I shivered, feeling his mouth over my mound, his tongue on my clit. My head fell back.

This was better than my dream. Better than anything I'd ever imagined. And when he hooked his fingers into my panties and dragged them down my legs before bringing his mouth back to my pussy, I knew there was no way to have ever imagined this without the experience. Behind my eyelids, I saw colors flashing, the stars shooting to and from their place in space. With his tongue, he drew another constellation, a private one, just for me, and when I orgasmed, it was his face that I saw painted in all those colors. I was still panting when I opened my eyes and saw him kneeling before me, just staring at me with his underwear still on. I sat up on my elbows and reached for the elastic, looking into his eyes, asking, pleading.

"We don't have to."

"Am I not your prize? To do with whatever you want?"

"I . . . " He let out a chuckle, glancing away briefly. "Having you here is prize enough, even if you will leave me, even if you will forget me."

"How could I forget you?" I sat up straight now, until we were nose to nose. "How could I forget this?"

"You will." His eyes were sad as he spoke and set a hand on the center of my chest. "You have before. You will again. It's okay, little witch. I'll settle for living inside of you. Deep in your bones. You'll always feel me there, with every breath you take."

I pulled him to me again, kissed his mouth with reverence, tugged his underwear off with his help. I pulled back and took him in, knowing my eyes were as wide as saucers. It wasn't like I had many men to compare him to, or any, for that matter, outside of the occasional porn search, but River was huge. I wrapped my hand around him, tugging gently. He moaned deeply, falling upon me and setting his closed fists on either side of me as his mouth found my neck.

"You'll kill me," he whispered. "You'll fucking kill me."

"I'll die if I do." I met his gaze.

His eyes widened at that. I didn't know where the words came from or why I said them. The only thing I knew was that in that moment, my chest felt like it would cave if I didn't have him inside me, and I knew that welcoming him would certainly change my life. River settled between my legs then, sliding his fingers inside me to coax me, but I didn't need to be further coaxed. He slid inside of me gently, slowly, keeping his dark eyes on mine as if to make sure I was okay, or maybe it was just to immortalize the moment. I couldn't breathe. Couldn't think. The only thing I could do was feel. Feel River inside me, his girth stretching me as he filled me. Every time it seemed like he was going to pull out, I held him tighter, wrapping my legs around his waist, my hands gripping his strong arms, all the while keeping my eyes on his, unable to look away. Like my first orgasm, and my dream, I felt it creep down my spine and spread through me. For a few seconds, it was as if everything was perfect, everything was light, everything was in color, and then he said my name.

"Penelope." He sighed, his forehead against mine as he pushed inside me deeper, faster. "Penelope."

My legs started to shake again, and this time, I came with a scream, saying his name in a chant that I couldn't imagine ever forgetting.

CHAPTER TWENTY-FOUR

"**C**AN WE JUST STAY HERE?" I TILTED MY HEAD TO LOOK AT River, who was smiling.

"I don't see why not." He kissed the top of my head. "As long as you don't mind the small toilet and lack of shower."

I sighed heavily. "I can do with the small toilet. The lack of shower, not so much."

"I thought so." He chuckled, the sound making me smile wider.

"How do you read my mind?"

"If I told you, you wouldn't believe me." He shifted, turning so we were face-to-face. "It only happens when I'm on the property. I can't go around reading minds when I'm anywhere else."

"I want to hear the story." I ran a finger over the side

of his face, marking each perfect bone contour. "I'll believe you."

"I'm not sure you will."

"Your mother drowned, didn't she?" I asked. "Is that what it's about?"

"In part." His smile faltered.

"We don't have to talk about it."

"I've never spoken to anyone about it before." He reached over and tucked a strand of loose hair behind my ear. "She wanted . . . she *needed* to get to one of the big islands, to Pan, or the DR or PR or Cuba, but Pan was closest and Pan was where her doctor was, so that was where she needed to be. My father, as you know, isn't allowed to step foot there. It's not so much that he doesn't want to go. He's tried, but he can't seem to move past a certain spot." River chuckled lightly. "A man who owns so much property and has so many investments, hotels, restaurants, nightclubs, and he can't step foot on the one piece of land that calls to him, that gave birth to him."

"It's a little sad when you say it like that," I whispered.

"Just a little?"

"Well, it's kind of difficult to feel sad for successful moguls."

"Your father, by all accounts, was a successful mogul."

"And I never felt sad for him." I raised an eyebrow. River smiled.

"My mother was allowed on Pan. She could get through whatever the invisible barriers were with no problem and visited her doctor there and even went out for dinner with friends. She wasn't a true Caliban, after all." He took a shaky breath. "She was pregnant with a baby girl. My little sister.

That night . . . " He swallowed. "That night, her contractions were getting stronger and because her delivery with me, just ten years prior, had been so quick, she decided to go to Pan."

"My God. You were ten when it happened?"

He nodded gravely. "I went with her. I knew my way around the boat, knew how to drive it. I was ten, but I'd grown up on all kinds of boats, sailing, fishing. Besides, my father was away on business and my mother was my . . . well, she was my best friend, really. We did everything together." He smiled sadly. "She called me her little sidekick and you'd think I'd be jealous about the child she was carrying, but I was excited. Finally, someone to play with, even if she would be an entire decade younger."

"River." I swallowed the lump in my throat and continued to listen.

"The fog wasn't heavy that day. The tree was blooming, the grass was green up until the spot where the grass turned to sand and then ocean water. It was nice out. Until it wasn't."

"What happened?"

"From what I remember, which is my ten-year-old memory, the winds suddenly picked up. I remember the fog, which had been clear just a second before, wrapping around us like a thick, dark blanket. I remember my mother screaming, yelling for me to secure my life vest. Hers wouldn't . . . she tried to put it on, but her belly—it just wouldn't budge." He shook his head. "Her body was never found."

"My God." I sat up with a gasp.

"When I came to, I was lying on the Devil's Chair." He was looking so intently at me, as if he needed me to pay close attention. "He asked me what I wanted. What my wish was. I said my mother, my baby sister. He laughed. Laughed." River shook his head in disbelief. "Then he told me that dead people couldn't resuscitate other dead people."

"What?" I blinked, trying to make sense of the nonsensical.

"So I asked to be brought back. I asked for life. Just life. I thought if I was alive he'd let me bring back my mother." He swallowed, glancing away, out the window, where the beautiful, clear skies had turned into a sudden torrential downpour. "He didn't. In exchange for my life, he tied me to him, to this island. To this house. I have bouts of freedom here and there, but I always have to come right back here."

I didn't know what to say, so I stayed silent. What could I say? That I was sorry? That I wished I could make it all better? I did, but I couldn't. I set my hand on his and squeezed.

"Sarah came along shortly after." He looked at me again. "I was in boarding school by then. I spent most of my life away from here, buried in books, parties, women. Anything to escape the memory and what I'd done, but every so often I . . . it's like a magnet. I feel like if I don't come home my body will be ripped apart."

"So that's why you came back? That's why you didn't finish medical school?"

"You can't really be on call at the hospital and also on the Devil's beck and call." He smiled softly. "It's not all bad, but still, I want the curse to be broken. I want it all gone."

"You want to be free," I whispered.

He nodded. "When my father sent word that I'd been chosen as Carnival host this year, I was once again magnetized, forced to come back, but all along, I knew who I'd pick."

"You couldn't have known I'd be here."

"But I did."

"Because of the accident."

"Unfortunately," he said, and looked genuinely sorry.

"How'd you know my grandmother told me to get the leaves?"

His eyes gleamed. "Your expression gave it away the minute you set eyes on the tree. Besides, I've heard stories about your grandmother's teas and potions."

"Good or bad?"

"My mother wasn't a fan. When she was pregnant with me, your grandmother wouldn't help her with a natural way to relieve back pain."

I sighed. "I've never understood the feud between our families."

"Most feuds are misunderstandings that feed off of other misunderstandings." He shrugged a shoulder. "It's not our problem."

"Why do you have so many scars?" I brought a hand up to his back and let my fingers run over them. His back was a mixture of scars and welts, some deeper than others.

"It's part of the curse. Each time those leaves are used to cure someone, I get a new scar on my back."

"Do they hurt?" I met his eyes, my fingers still running over them.

"When they happen, yes. It hasn't in some time."

I pressed my lips together and thought about my grand-mother, who used those leaves so much that she'd run out of them. I wondered if she knew about this curse, about River's scars. I wondered if she understood what she was doing to him every time she helped someone else or if she even cared. I hated seeing him like this. I hated knowing all of those things had happened to him and that somehow my blood was tied to it.

"What will you do once the curse is broken?" I asked after a moment.

"If it's ever broken," he said.

"It will be. What will you do?"

"I don't know." He shot me a secretive smile. "Probably become an ER doctor somewhere. Maybe in Florida."

"That wasn't a dream, was it?"

"It was. I just happened to experience it with you." He grinned. "You have a very dirty mind, little witch. I like it."

"I don't normally." I felt myself blush deeply. "I've always been a prude."

"You say that like it's a bad thing."

"Sometimes it feels like it is. My friends are all so . . . free." I frowned. "I've never really thought much about sex. Not until . . ."

"Until what?" His eyes darkened.

"You know what." I bit my lip, hating the heat on my face, all over my body. "You can probably read my mind right now."

"I'd rather hear the words come from your mouth."

"Until you. You bring this out in me."

"Do I?" He reached for me, carrying me onto his lap so that my legs were spread on either side of him and our faces were close together.

Even as I leaned in to kiss him, he was looking at me with such longing it nearly broke my heart. I thought of what he'd said earlier, how I'd forgotten him once and he knew I'd forget him again, and it killed me to think that only one of us would carry this memory forever. If that was the case, I'd make it worthwhile.

CHAPTER TWENTY-FIVE

H E DROVE FAST, DESPITE THE BUMPY, UNEVEN TERRAIN. Meanwhile, my heart was in my throat as I held on to my seat, as if holding on to anything could save me if the car careened off the road and hit the mountain, or worse.

"Maybe slow down a bit," I said, finally, because acting brave was cool, but staying alive was much more important.

"Sorry." He shifted gears and slowed down. I let out the breath I seemed to have been holding since we left the Manor.

"Not wearing a seatbelt can kill you." I glanced over at him in time to catch his mouth pull up. "Driving like that and not wearing a seatbelt will surely kill you though."

"I know."

"Yet you do it."

"Let's just say I've spent the majority of my life testing how far I could push the envelope."

"As much as I can . . . sort of understand that, considering you sold your soul to the Devil and all, I don't think it's fair to push the envelope with me in the car."

"You're right." He reached for my hand, bringing it up to his lips. "You're right. I'm sorry."

"It's okay. Just stop trying to kill me."

He chuckled; it was a deep laugh that struck me all wrong. I had a question on the tip of my tongue, but then I saw light in front of us and my voice remained in my throat. It was a village, a town, with streets and street lamps and structures. There were people spilling onto the street from bars, from whatever businesses were up. River pulled up to the sidewalk and parked the car, turning to me.

"You weren't kidding when you said there was a whole town," I said. "Who are all of these people?"

"Some you met at the party the other night. Others are here for fun. All are the lost souls that are so often talked about when people bring up Dolos."

"But they're . . . alive, right?"

"Very much so." His eyes crinkled. "Does a soul ever die?"

"I'm not sure." I blinked. "You subscribe to the notion that nothing dies."

"It's what I know." He shrugged a shoulder and looked out the front windshield. I followed his gaze. "Most of these are brothels, bars, places they can come and gamble in, get-rich-quick schemes."

"Interesting." I looked at him again. "Do you spend a lot of time here?"

"Hell no." His gaze whipped to mine. "I used to, when I was younger. It gets old fast, like most vices do."

"Except for smoking apparently."

"Well, that's an addictive habit." He smiled.

"So is gambling. And prostitution. And whatever else is going on here." I looked outside again, where a scandalously dressed woman was laughing at something a man in a suit was saying to her. "Why haven't I ever heard of Dolos being such a hot spot for seedy things? You'd think it would be as popular as Las Vegas."

"What happens in Vegas stays in Vegas. What happens in Dolos never happened." He raised an eyebrow.

"I thought they said that about Miami."

"Everyone in Miami has a cell phone. Cell phones don't work here."

"Well, shit." I sat back in my seat. "How'd they get here? The water hasn't risen around the island."

"Helicopters, private planes, some docked their yachts in Pan Island last week."

"Jesus." My eyes found a familiar face outside, a billionaire who was always in the tabloids. The lifestyles of the rich and the famous indeed.

"Do you want to get down?"

"Not really. I'm okay with just driving around."

River started driving. He pointed out the window frequently as we passed things like the market, clothing stores, and hair salons. The entirety of the town took up two blocks, nothing more. There was one row of townhouses and one row of bars and brothels. That was it.

"What about the rest of the island?"

"It remains untouched for the most part. There are some vacation homes on the shore, but not many. This is why some people call it the Devil's Playground," River said. "It's not because they understand that he actually resides here."

"Where does he live?"

"Everywhere." River met my gaze as he drove and the intensity of it was impossible to ignore. "If you believe the stories, which I do, he was banished from Heaven and exiled to Earth, and isn't that perfect? Where better to have someone with questionable morals exist than a place where everyone is looking for something to give them purpose, without realizing their purpose was planted inside of them all along?"

I thought about that long after we got back to the Manor. Long after we made love again before falling asleep. I'd always pushed thoughts about the Devil and the curse aside, never really knowing why I was so completely against any of it being real, but now I understood. I tried to ignore it and speak against it because it made me uncomfortable, but discomfort often led to change and I was open to that.

CHAPTER TWENTY-SIX

HOOKED A FINGER INTO THE CANDLEHOLDER AND WALKED OUTSIDE of the bedroom, careful to shut the door quietly behind me. I couldn't sleep and River, who hardly seemed to, was sound asleep tonight. The candlelight created a shadow on the walls as I walked down the stairs, holding the skirt of the silk robe I wore carefully so that I wouldn't trip. When I reached the foyer, I half expected to see one of the staff members dusting and cleaning, as they always seemed to be, but it was dark, desolate, only the sound of my breathing audible. I wasn't sure what I was doing down here alone, but something had called me to get out of bed and come. I stepped into the study and stood in the center of the room, my eyes on the stained glass in front of me.

"The house really was beautiful once." The voice came from the door. I gasped and swirled around. It was Mayra standing there. She walked inside, leaving the door open behind her. She was still wearing the same outfit she always wore, black from head to toe, long skirt dragging. Could it be that she slept in it?

"I couldn't sleep," I said.

"The irony of you wearing white tonight." Mayra smiled as she walked past me and looked at the shelves. I felt myself blush. Was she referring to me having sex with River? She continued speaking before I could get a word in. "I never sleep. It's such a shame. This library used to be a source of entertainment."

"Really?"

"Really." She stopped walking and turned to me. "What woke you?"

"I don't know. I guess my mind just won't stop running."

"You're trying to figure out a way to break the curse."

"How do you know?" My hand tightened on the candleholder.

"River isn't the only one indebted to the Devil." Her mouth moved into a small smile. "I can help you break it."

"Why should I trust you?"

"You don't have to, but if you want to help River this may be your only hope." She stepped closer. "Besides, I want my freedom as well. We all do."

"What do I have to do?"

"Just talk to him. Hear him out."

"Who?"

"You know who." Her eyes seemed to shine in the darkness, almost looking like the fire in my hand.

"How would I talk to him? Where? When?"

"I'll take you to him if you want." She started walking to the door and glanced over her shoulder. "Are you coming?"

I followed her. Despite the candle burning in my hand, my body grew cold as we walked through the halls. She led me outside and I was certain she'd take me to the Devil's Chair, but she didn't go to the cobblestones or the driveway. She just walked the yard, past the tree, and continued on. I looked over my shoulder and was surprised to see the house much farther than I thought it would be. I looked up at the windows in the attic, the place River felt was truly his. Everything was dark. Only half of the candle was left to burn when I looked at it again. I could hear the ocean from here. I could smell the water, the wet sand.

"How much farther?" I asked.

"Not much." She glanced over at me. "I don't look like this to everyone, you know."

"Like what?"

"The way you see me."

"I don't understand what you mean."

"You find me old and haggard, no?"

"No. I can't imagine you're much older than I am."

"Hm." She let out a laugh. "You must be jealous of me." She reached into the pockets of her dress and brought out a box of cigarettes, offering them to me before taking one out and lighting it when I shook my head.

"I'm not jealous of you."

"River used to smoke." She tilted her head back and blew out the smoke in her mouth. "He looked so sexy whilst doing it. So sexy."

I swallowed, hating that she was right and jealousy spread through me. He'd said they weren't lovers, and I figured that much had to be true now, but that didn't mean they'd never been together. That didn't mean she didn't want him still.

That didn't mean she wouldn't have him after I was gone, and that was the thought that hurt me most. My days here were numbered and I knew that if I didn't leave when I was supposed to, my mother wouldn't survive without the leaves.

"I don't like cigarette smoke and I'm allergic."

"Shame." She continued smoking. "Since this is a quid pro quo, sort of speak, I'll let you in on a secret, you see me young. Men, the ones who are especially tired of their wives see me the same, maybe younger, probably sexier. Men like River? They see me for what I am. A one-hundred-year-old bitter lady who just wants her freedom."

"One hundred?" I stopped walking. She did as well.

"One hundred and two." She turned her head to me with a smile that didn't reach her eyes.

"That's impossible."

"Is it?" She laughed and fell into a fit of coughs before tossing the cigarette aside. She turned back around and kept walking. "I was here when this land and that one were still connected."

"How?" I walked faster to catch up. "How?"

"I asked for too much. He has a damning sense of humor."

"What did you ask for?"

"The man I loved to love me in return."

I frowned. "That doesn't seem like too much."

"He was married to my sister. The only way I could have him was if she was no longer here." Mayra met my gaze. "It's a long story, one that I regret every single waking moment. There are millions of men in the world. Millions. I could have left this island. I could have met another." She exhaled a deep breath, shaking her head.

"So what happened?"

"My sister set a curse on me, on this island, on the Calibans."

"Are you a Caliban?"

Mayra laughed. She stopped walking and faced me. The candle shook forcefully in my hand as I took her in this time. She looked different, her skin darker, the sockets around her eyes even hollower, but more terrifying than anything else, she looked just like my grandmother. I swallowed, taking one step back, then another. It could be a coincidence. A lot of women on Pan and the surrounding islands looked like my grandmother. We were all Caribbean, after all. Something about Mayra's expression, however, begged me to recognize her.

"You see me," she said. "Finally."

"I don't understand." My voice shook as the candle spilled out of my hand and toppled over the grass.

"Stupid girl." Mayra threw something on the candle quickly, dust, sand—whatever it was ensured that the light was gone. "Are you trying to burn us all to death?"

"Are you a Guzman?"

"I am. I was. I denounced that name long ago, just like my sister denounced me."

"Who's your sister?" I could barely get the question out, my voice a whisper against the crashing waves.

"Maria Guzman."

My grandmother? I brought my hands up to my mouth, cupping it as if to keep from screaming, but there was no scream lodged in my throat, there was nothing other than shock, and shock seldom held a sound. I stared at Mayra. Mayra Guzman, a woman I'd never even heard of, but was my grandmother's sister. I searched deep in my memories for that name and came up blank. I searched for old pictures, anything that I might have seen and overlooked, but there was nothing.

"I held you when you were a baby. You won't remember. I watched you as you walked home at night. You won't remember."

"The yellow eyes," I whispered.

She pressed her lips together and nodded.

"Why did you watch me? Why did you visit after you'd been banished? How?"

"Carnival. It's the only time of year we can roam as we please." She smiled sadly. "Men, like River, are able to travel and roam the world as they please until it's time for, as you call him, the Devil, to collect. Women aren't as lucky. He is a man after all." She pursed her lips. "During Carnival, I visit my sister, though I stopped letting her see me years ago."

"Don't you hate her for what she did?" I felt myself frown. I know I would and with everything I'd heard about her while here, I definitely was questioning what I thought I knew.

"I did in the beginning. When the island broke apart. When we were physically banished. I learned to forgive her. It was either that or fully give into his will and I wouldn't lose more of myself to him."

"Why are the Calibans involved?"

"Nicolas was best friends with Wilfred the first and was counting on Wilfred to help us be together. Of course, unbeknownst to us, Maria was already pregnant with your father."

"She set the curse when she found out," I whispered.

"Wilfred was driving Nicolas over to the Manor that night. He'd packed a bag and left a note. Maria must have suspected because she showed up before they even arrived. I wasn't there, but she'd laid traps, worked a fire, and had already started burning my belongings, his belongings. Wilfred tried to intervene but only made matters worse. She took her anger out on him. Threw torches at his back, the fire burned through his clothes. It was awful." Mayra's voice seemed far away now, as if she was experiencing everything, but there was no emotion in her voice as she recounted the scene. "By the time I got there, Nicolas had left. To this day, I don't know how or why he left."

"Maybe he wanted her to calm down. Maybe he loved her." Even though I didn't remember my grandfather, I'd seen pictures of them together and they seemed happy.

"He despised Maria. They were only married because our father and his had come to an agreement. Marriage was still a business transaction back then."

"She loved him," I said. "Otherwise, she wouldn't have cursed a friend or her own sister."

"She was jealous of me." Mayra laughed. "It doesn't matter. That night, I bargained with the Devil and he turned me into this. I can't die. I can't sleep. I can't find peace. I just roam. I roam and I sleep with married men, lonely men. Some I send back to their wives, changed, broken, looking for me in the woods most nights. Others, the terrible ones, I feed to him."

"Is that what you're doing now?" I licked my lips. "Feeding me to him?"

"It's the only way. It's the only way to break free of this."

I nodded, looking into the darkness, closing my eyes to listen to the waves. Somehow, I'd suspected it would come to this. That I was too tied to this land to ever leave it. I hadn't made peace with it, but I'd find a way to before I met the Devil. It was the only way, and in exchange, my mother would live, River would live. I opened my eyes and looked at Mayra. Her eyes were now glowing, as if the candle had burned into them. I wasn't afraid, not really, but seeing that made me shiver.

"Will he kill me?" I asked.

"No. I suspect he'll make a bargain. It's what he does. It's all he knows."

"Why me?"

"Why not?" There was a sadness in her tone. She reached out and grabbed my arm, not forcefully, but with enough grip that I knew to start walking beside her again. "You're the purest thing that's stepped foot here in a long time. An uncorrupt soul is a rare find."

"What will happen to you?" I wobbled, nearly tripping on a rock. She held me tighter so that I wouldn't fall. "Will you be free?"

"I don't know. I don't know what freedom looks like. I never have." She let go of my arm when it felt like we reached steady, flat ground. She took out another cigarette and lit it. "How was it, life far away from the island?"

"It was nice." I eyed her warily. "Maybe your freedom will buy you time away from here."

"Maybe." She seemed to smile at that.

Panic rose deep inside me when the terrain switched from damp grass and rocks to wet sand. Wet sand meant the water was much closer than I originally thought, and with the week coming to an end it also meant it would rise soon. Maybe Mayra's plan was to kill me herself. Maybe all of this was a ploy to take revenge on my grandmother for what she'd done. Finally, she stopped walking and reached down to pick something up. A torch, which she lit in one swift motion before handing it to me. I took it and carried it in front of my face to make out my surroundings.

We were standing in front of a massive black rock. A cave, I realized, upon seeing an opening. Mayra walked closer. I followed, walking slowly behind her. She reached up and untied her hair from its usual bun. It unraveled swiftly as it came down, covering her already black attire with more black. Unlike my grandmother's tight curls, Mayra had long, straight, black hair. *La Ciguapa*'s hair. The thought made me shiver. She walked inside the cave. I idled for a moment, taking another look over my shoulder, toward the Manor, which was at such a distance I could barely make it out. And then, taking a deep breath and saying a short prayer to God, the God my grandmother always hoped I'd believe in, I walked inside.

CHAPTER TWENTY-SEVEN

RIVER

H E'D SLEPT. A DEEP SLUMBER THAT SEEMED TO NEVER END, BUT something woke him. Penelope. Penelope walking into the Mouth of the Devil. River sat up in bed with a gasp, his chest heaving. Mayra. He scrambled out of bed, fighting sheets that tied up his feet, begging him to stay. He shoved his legs into the first pair of pants he found and grabbed a T-shirt and pulled it over his head. He was already sprinting out the door when his eyes caught a pair of sneakers and he grabbed those too, taking the stairs two at a time.

"What's wrong?" The voice came from his father.

"Penelope's at the Mouth of the Devil." He yanked his sneakers on and headed to the back of the house.

"If she's already there, there's nothing you can do," his father called out.

"Let him be, Will." That was Sarah's soothing voice.

"I have to try," River shouted as he exited the house.

He had to try.

It was all he could say. All he could do. His father wasn't wrong. If Penelope was already there, River stood no chance. He had nothing else left to bargain. His soul wasn't his. It hadn't been since he was ten and even though he'd longed to be free of the invisible chains that kept him tied to this house, to him, he also knew what it would take. A pure heart. A wholesome soul. *Her.* River couldn't stomach it. He'd complied with everything that was asked of him most of the time, but this, he couldn't bear this. She wasn't meant to be tethered. It was that thought that made him run faster through the grass at the back of his house. The grass didn't grow much here, though no one really knew why. River had always been told the island didn't allow for new life, and that extended to the grass itself. The land used up all of its resources to replenish the Tree of Life each year and once the life faded from it and the leaves dried up, all of its energy went right back to the ocean and its angry waves. When he reached the sand, he was surprised to feel it wet beneath his feet. That wasn't supposed to happen until tomorrow evening. The realization made him run harder.

He was almost to the cave when he hit a wall. His body shot into the air and was thrown back against the sand. It took River a moment to recover from the impact. A figure was walking toward him when he came to, blinking slowly as white and black dots blurred his vision. He stood up shakily, trying to find equilibrium to keep going. Even through the blurred vision, River knew it was him, the Devil himself. Though he didn't like the name Devil, he'd never given himself a name, and River's lack of interest for the occult left him with only that word to call him.

"You're too late."

"No." River stepped forward once more, chest filled with dread, with pain. "Please."

"You've pled your bargain once, boy. You were brought back. Wasn't that enough?"

"No." He shook his head, looking beyond the figure, toward the caves. He couldn't make anything out. "Please," he said again. "I'll give you anything."

"You don't have anything left to give." He chuckled deeply, wickedly, a sound that had always made River want to run for the hills.

"I'll make a trade. I'll do your bidding, no matter what you ask of me. Just set her free."

"Again, that is not something that interests me. I have others doing my bidding. You think you're the only one?" The figure swayed, like smoke, like air, like fire.

"There must be something." River held his breath. There *had* to be something.

"Maybe there is," he said after a long moment. "Maybe there is."

CHAPTER TWENTY-EIGHT

PENELOPE

I**T WAS ALWAYS LEADING TO THIS, WASN'T IT? T**HE ISLAND GIVETH and taketh away. Not the island. I'd always thought it was the island that decided that, as if it were some sort of god. We'd built lives and worshiped it like pagans, and for what? To die anyway, in the end. We used happiness as a bargaining chip, but we never won. How could one win against the Devil? It seemed impossible. I thought of River and my lip began to tremble. I hadn't even gotten a chance to say goodbye. I hadn't gotten a chance to kiss him again, to be held by him.

My chest felt like it might explode in its cavity, like I might bleed out from within. The shards of broken seashells underneath my bare feet were a welcome distraction from that pain. Mayra grabbed my hand and pulled me to walk faster. I wasn't surprised that she wasn't complaining about it. She was used to being barefoot, used to taking pain in a way that I wasn't. After all, I had been shielded from it for years. Shielded from the pain and anguish that my memories would have provided me. Shielded from the pain falling in love brought with it, because there was no falling in love without letting go. There was no use in denying or hiding it now. I'd fallen in love with River Caliban. Maybe I was as stupid as my father once said I was. Maybe I was as crazy as they called my grandmother. It didn't matter though. No amount of warnings would have kept me away from him and no amount of walls could have stayed put between us. It was an impossibility in a series of them from the beginning. We'd both known that. Mayra stopped walking. I stopped with her, doubling over to cry over the pain—in my chest, on the pads of my feet—and glanced up at her, wiping wet hair from my equally wet face. It was so dark, the fog so heavy, the wind had gotten stronger and the rain was coming down hard now. I could barely see her.

"He knows." She looked up at the dark sky above us.

"Who knows what?"

She started walking again and stopped again just a few feet away, where a boat swayed in the ocean water, tied to a piece of wood buried in the sand.

"We're going by boat?" I took a step back, biting down on my lip to keep from crying out in pain.

"How else would you suggest we get from one island to another with the tide rising this quickly and the rain not stopping?"

"I wouldn't suggest it at all." I looked around. "There has to be another way."

"There is no other way." Mayra was untying the rope

now and holding it in her hand to make sure it wouldn't go anywhere, the way someone holds a horse in place. I looked back toward the Manor, saw lights flickering. My heart grew heavier. River was awake. I felt that truth in my bones. He was awake and looking for me. Would he come over here and search? Did he know what I'd done?

"You need to leave," Mayra said, breaking into my thoughts. "We need to leave now."

I bit my lip and nodded even though I didn't agree. I knew I had to. I knew there was no other way. As I walked to the boat, I swore I felt hands helping me step into it. Mayra handed me a paddle. I held it tightly in my fists. A wave came and rocked us. I let go of the paddle and held the sides of the boat. We were going to die out here, but if we didn't, if we managed to get to the other side, I could save my mother. I could save her and break the curse and even though I didn't believe in curses I believed in River and if my leaving meant he'd be safe, so be it.

"I'll paddle. Save your strength. You'll need it."

I nodded, holding on to the paddle on my lap again. As she paddled, Mayra prayed. I'd never heard a witch pray before, so I leaned in and shut my eyes to listen. *Our Father, who art in heaven . . .* my eyes popped open, only to find hers closed as she paddled, her arms moving at a steady pace against the strong current. She said the prayer again, on a never-ending loop, the way my grandmother did when she was praying the rosary. Another wave hit us and my instant panic turned to sobs. What if I didn't make it to the other side? I'd never been afraid of death, but I didn't want to drown. I squeezed my eyes shut, breathing through another wave that made the boat unsteady, and as my eyes were closed, I joined Mayra in prayer. We said two more Our Fathers before she stopped. I opened my eyes and looked at her.

"We're almost there," she shouted over the water. "You'll need to start paddling now. Promise me that you won't stop."

"Why would I stop?" I shouted back.

"Just . . . promise." She held my eyes in a serious stare, one I couldn't tear my gaze from.

I nodded. "I won't stop paddling."

The wave that came next careened the boat into the air. I gripped onto the sides of it and squeezed my eyes shut with a scream as my stomach dipped, as if I was in a freefall, a roller coaster with no end point. When the boat crashed down, I opened my eyes and grabbed my paddle quickly to make sure it didn't go overboard. When I looked up at Mayra, she was no longer there. Her paddle was, but there was no sign of her.

"Mayra?" I turned and looked behind me. "Mayra!"

She was gone. Gone. I looked around anxiously, calling out her name, screaming it as loud as I could. Had the wave taken her? Had the curse?

"Fuck you, Satan," I yelled as I started to shake. "Fuck you."

I began to cry loudly as I paddled. The water felt so heavy beneath me, too strong to move, but I had to. I'd promised Mayra I would keep paddling and I would. I thought of River, and my mother, and everyone who was depending on me getting back to Pan, and paddled harder. My arms started burning, my shoulders aching, but I kept going. The waves lessened. The fog lifted ever so slightly. The boat hit something that made me rear forward and fall onto the seat Mayra was supposed to be in. When I looked up, I realized I'd hit sand. Palm trees lined the perimeter behind me and I knew I was back at Pan. Either that or I'd made it all the way to the Dominican Republic, but it didn't matter. I was somewhere. I climbed out of the boat, my arms aching, my feet throbbing. The gown I wore was soaked and weighed me down, but I swept up the bottom and wrung it out with the little energy I had left. I walked one, two, maybe three whole steps on the hot sand before my knees gave out on me and I passed out.

When I came to, I was sitting on the Devil's Chair. I blinked, my eyes adjusting to the light that the sun provided from behind the clouds.

"Will you make your wish now?" the voice asked. "Who will you choose? Your boyfriend or your mother? Or does you being back on Pan mean you've made that choice?" There was a dark amusement in his voice and I hated that I'd ever associated it with River's.

My shoulders began to shake as I sat there, not saying any words, careful not to think anything. I kept my mind blank, lest not to make him run with any ideas and grant anything I didn't wish to be granted.

"What do you want?" I asked, a wail. "What do you want?"

"Make a wish."

I closed my eyes and then I did.

I had no recollection of walking home or getting there. I just knew that with each step, my heart grew heavier. I thought of River when I stopped in front of my door. If I went inside, would I forget him? Isn't that what I should have wanted? He'd tormented me, practically conned me into staying with him, and just when I didn't think I had one more thing left to give, he took my heart. That sounded like someone worth forgetting. I felt a poke inside my ribs, a jab, a reminder. I laughed loudly, shoulders shaking. I crashed down on my knees and started crying again. Fucking River.

The door of the house opened. Through wet eyes, I could see my grandmother standing by the door in a flower muumuu and hair rollers covering her head.

"You did it." She rushed over to me, taking the leaves from my hands and picking me up from the ground.

Inside, she got to work, making her tea for Mami. I watched numbly. She hadn't even taken another glance at me. Hadn't even cared what I had given to get these damn leaves. I realized she'd always been like that. She cared about herself and sure she'd cared about her family, but at what cost?

"It's your fault the curse exists." I swallowed.

She stopped mashing leaves and glanced at me. "You met Mayra."

"How could you do that to your own sister?"

"Did she tell you what she did? She wished for my death."

"And then the Devil turned around and told you about it so you wished for something worse," I said. "You always told me to stay away from there. To stay away from them, from the Chair, and all the while you were the cause of all of this pain."

She glanced away, looking down at the leaves, and continued mashing. She was quiet as she picked them up and set them in the boiling pan. Quiet as she prepared it in a mug.

Quiet as she walked it out of the kitchen and over to my mother's room. I cried again as I sat there. I felt like a different person in this house. It's funny what knowledge does to someone. What forgiveness brings. I'd come here looking for both of those things from my grandmother, my mother. I didn't know I wouldn't find it here at all. I didn't know I'd find it in the one place I should've never gone looking, but I did. I found especially that the forgiveness I so desperately was seeking had to come from myself, not anyone else.

CHAPTER TWENTY-NINE

RIVER

"IF SHE'D STAYED LONG ENOUGH SHE COULD HAVE LIFTED THIS curse. She could have cured this house. I felt it, felt her presence lighting the way," Sarah said.

"She chose to save her mother. We can't fault her for that."

"A mother who did her no good?" Sarah shook her head. "A mother who shunned and turned her back on her?"

River glanced over at Sarah. "A mother, nonetheless."

"Your father won't survive the night," she responded. "You don't look so well yourself."

"I know." He did.

He knew he'd be gone soon. He knew how this worked. His father would die, Penelope's mother would live. River would die and Penelope would live. It was the bargain he'd made, after all. Two souls for the price of one. He would have bargained that of Gia Guzman's, but the Devil didn't want wretched souls, only pure ones, and even though River had done his share of bad shit in his day, he'd done half of those in the Devil's name, and asked for penance on the other half.

Technically, he was a fucking saint.

He laughed at that.

CHAPTER THIRTY

RIVER

THE HOUSE SHOOK VIGOROUSLY. HE HADN'T SLEPT IN TWO nights, but even he knew he wasn't fabricating what he felt. He clicked the mouse and shut down the computer. Even as he clicked the button, the irony wasn't lost on him. More likely than not, he wasn't going to survive whatever came next. He knew that because he asked for it and he felt the Devil smile at the request. Sick bastard. River knew he didn't need him. His back was covered in welts and scars. He was running out of space and the Devil liked blank canvases. So yeah, he was pretty sure he'd die. The house shook again, harder this time. He ran out of the study and found his father standing in the foyer.

"I sent Sarah away. You should go."

"Why didn't you go with her?" River shot him a bewildered look. "Why are you still here?"

"I'll die here." His father smiled. It wasn't happy or sad. It was the smile of a man who'd made peace with his destiny. "You should go."

"I'm not just going to leave you."

The house shook again, and this time, the chandelier hooked into the thirty-foot ceiling in the center of the foyer came crashing down, the crystals spattering everywhere. River put an arm around his father to shield him from the crystals that bounced in their direction. Wilfred had never been one of those fathers who showed much emotion, rarely hugging River or kissing him. He often just squeezed his shoulder and smiled, and most of the time that was enough. Sarah had been the opposite. Though she wasn't his mother, she'd been very motherly toward him, always there to kiss him and hug him when he got home, always there to encourage him and smile when he needed her to. He smiled now, thinking of her safety, of her freedom, finally.

River took hold of his father's hand and walked him to the back of the house, toward the Tree of Life. It was a longshot, but *maybe*. Anything was possible. His father was walking slower than usual, but River pushed on, gripping his hand tighter, walking harder against the gusts of wind. This wasn't normal. The day leading up to the water rising again was always nice, the final nice day they had until the gloom settled again. It was never this. It had never been this. River wondered if his mood had anything to do with that. If the fact that he was mourning his loss was causing all of this, the loss of the woman he loved. The loss of what might have been, had he not been tethered to such a despicable being. He glanced at the garage door. If they could make it there and race to the helipad, he could get them out of here. But he still needed the leaves. The ground beneath them shook again, this time forming clear fault lines around them.

"Let go," his father said, trying to pull his hand away from his. "You need to let go."

"I can't." River felt his chest squeeze as he looked at his father, who seemed to be aging right before his eyes.

"You need to let go now, River. You can't save us all."

"I can't save anyone." He blinked hard against the gusts, trying to keep his eyes on his father's.

"You can save yourself."

"If I save myself she dies. You know how this works."

My father nodded slowly, eyes turned sad. It was why he sent Sarah away knowing she'd survive, even though he wouldn't. It was why he was so absolute in his decision. Staying, dying, giving into the inevitable, was the only way to save the woman he loved. And so, River didn't let go of his father's hand, even as they reached the Tree of Life. Even as they sat beneath it and looked out into emptiness. He heard the ocean waves nearing, but they weren't calm and docile as they always were this time of year. They were charging, ready for war, ready to cause destruction. Wilfred lay his head on his son's shoulder and closed his eyes, letting out a soft sigh. River set his head on top of his father's and gripped a chunk of soil beneath him, touching the leaves that had fallen from the tree, and he shut his eyes as he watched the Manor collapse and awaited doom. He could swear he heard the Devil's laugh even now.

CHAPTER THIRTY-ONE

"**D**ID YOU HEAR?" DEE ASKED. SHE SOUNDED OUT OF BREATH as I answered the phone.

"Hear what?" I looked at the time. I felt like I'd slept three days, but in reality, it had been . . . "Holy shit. I think I slept twenty-four hours straight."

"Never mind that. Dolos is gone."

I shot straight up in bed. "What?"

"It's gone. The fog is gone. The island is . . . gone."

My heart leaped out of my chest. "No, no, no, no, no. I have to call you back." I hung up and ran into the bathroom.

When I was finished getting dressed, I ran out of my bedroom and into the kitchen. Wela was there, distributing leaves and setting them in different metal containers.

"Your mother is awake." She looked up at me with a smile.

"Dolos Island is gone." I felt like I was out of breath.

"I heard."

"How? Why?"

"I . . ." She stopped what she was doing and turned to me. "I don't know. Does it matter? The darkness has been lifted once and for all."

I stared at her for a long moment, then shook my head and ran out the door, climbing on my Vespa and revving it as hard as I could. I got as far as Dolly's bar before I had to stop driving because there were too many people on the street to dodge. News cameras, reporters, tourists, locals, people everywhere. Everyone was talking about Dolos Island and what could have possibly happened. I ran to Dolly's, heading straight to her behind the bar.

"Where's River?"

"How would I know?" She took a step back and eyed me up and down.

"Has he called? Did he say anything about his apartment? Did he—"

She put a hand up to shut me up and reached behind her for an envelope. She handed it to me and watched as I ripped it open. There was a key inside it. I glanced up at her.

"What's this?"

"From River," she said, smiling. For a split second, I felt joy, but then she added, "He said he wanted you to keep it."

I swallowed, unable to fight the tears that welled up in my eyes. I blinked rapidly and walked past her, toward the stairs in the back, stomping up until I reached the third floor and then the apartment. I unlocked and opened it, shutting and locking it behind me. It was empty, and it was then that I began to cry. The furniture was still there, but there was no sound, no movement, and . . . I ran to the bedroom . . . it was empty. *Why would he leave me his apartment? Why would he leave me?* I paced it. I went up to the window and looked out over the sea of people. The ocean was back, the waves had come well into the iron gates, flooding the buildings that stood near it. Even the Devil's Chair seemed to be gone. My heart squeezed even more so. There was no Manor, no Dolos Island beyond the gates. Only water. It was an impossibility. I cried harder as the word came to mind, and then, I climbed in bed and closed my eyes to hang onto the smell of him as I wept.

Movement woke me up. I gasped when I saw him. Threw my arms around him when he neared. Buried my face in his neck and inhaled him, squeezing harder.

"I didn't even get to say goodbye. I didn't say goodbye." It hurt when I spoke the words, emotion clogging up my throat to the point of pain.

"It's okay," he whispered against my hair, holding me tight.

"Is this a dream?" I pulled back.

His smile was sad. His nod was brief. I shut my eyes and let the tears cascade down my cheeks. His fingers wiped them away and I opened my eyes to meet his gaze.

"I'm only gone physically, little witch." His lip turned up. "You'll still carry me inside you, deep within your bones."

"I want you here." I shook my head, tears continuously spilling. "In front of me. For real."

He kept smiling. "One day, when you're alone and afraid, I'll poke you from within and you'll feel me there, and then you won't feel so alone, so afraid anymore."

"I don't want that. I want you here." I cried harder. My shoulders shook. Tears fell, snot loosened. I didn't care. I wiped my face with the back of my hand. "I want you here."

"You'll have me here." He kissed the tip of my nose, my cheek, my lips.

I returned the kiss harder, more frantically, and undressed him as he undressed me. I made my way down his body, dragging my lips on every etch and every plane. He gripped my hair when I kneeled between his legs. I glanced up at him, reveling in that dark gaze. The weight of his lust propelled me into action, pulling him into my mouth and sucking, licking, moving until he groaned and gripped me tighter. He yanked me off of him and pulled me up with the same hand that was just encouraging the foreplay, and slammed his mouth against mine, unleashing his tongue into my mouth. His other hand found my breasts, my nipples, my clit, and rubbed as he mouth-fucked me, his fingers in my hair gripping to the point of pain as I cried out, soaking his other fingers. He let go of my hair to hold me by the waist and pull me on top of him. It started out hard—him slamming into me, punishing me, but then he turned me so that my back was flat on the mattress and he hovered over me, looking into my eyes and sliding in and out of me painstakingly slowly, as if memorizing every second of the moment, unwilling to let it go. I remembered it was a dream, and that maybe, possibly, River might be experiencing it as well. I brought a hand up to his face as he continued to move inside of me.

"I love you," I whispered. "I'm sorry I couldn't save you."

He kissed me then, deeply, with an ardor and longing I knew I'd have for him as long as I lived, and when we found ecstasy, he smiled down at me.

"Your love sustained me and made up for a lifetime of loneliness," he said. "I'll love you for eternity."

And then, he was gone. I gasped, sitting up in bed, sweating, and when I looked down, I wasn't wearing any clothes.

"River?" I scrambled out of bed. "River?"

No one answered.

CHAPTER THIRTY-TWO

A few days later

"I**T'S A MIRACLE," THE PRIEST SAID. "GIA GUZMAN HAS MADE A** full recovery."

The church cheered. I clapped, but I wasn't really there. I looked out the window I was sitting beside and saw someone out in the cemetery. I blinked. Mayra? I stood quickly and walked to the back of the church, not worrying about the people looking at me as I went. They all thought I was crazy anyway. Half of them had told me to leave the island. That I was a devil worshipper. Never mind that I was the reason they were still alive and thriving. Never mind that they depended on the very leaves I brought back for that. I rushed to where I'd seen Mayra, but there was no one there. I looked around, left to right, right to left, and found nothing. With a sigh, I walked back toward the church. As I walked, I looked down at the unpaved road beneath my feet and saw track marks. Bare feet. They were all facing one way. *La Ciguapa*. I looked up in the opposite direction of which they came and saw a woman standing at the edge, where the tombstones met the forest. A young woman, dark, much younger than Mayra could ever be. *Fabiola*. She smiled at me, a bright smile, and bowed deeply. I didn't begin to cry, but the sob stayed in my chest, heavy, making it difficult to breathe.

Divers had been surrounding the area where Dolos once stood, but it was gone. The Calibans, the Devil's Chair, the seedy town, and its people. Just gone. I'd done a ton of Google searches on it and found very little being reported. It seemed that news of Dolos and Pan Island only made it as far as the surrounding islands and even then it wasn't top news. The people in Puerto Rico, Cuba, Haiti, Jamaica, and the Dominican Republic had bigger things to worry about, taking care of the aftermath of their own natural disasters.

"Is everything okay?" That was my mother.

I turned and nodded at her. She was wearing a black dress that hit her just beneath her knee, black heels, and her black hair up in a nice bun. She held out a hand for me, which I took, and walked back to the church.

"I hate that you're leaving," she said.

"I can't stay. Too many things have happened."

"I wish you'd talk about them."

I smiled, squeezing her hand. She and everyone else. I hadn't given Dee or Martín any details. I simply said I was grateful to be home. I smiled and offered both of them some of my grandmother's famous tea when they came over. I'd set the intention. They'd forget where I'd been. They'd forget who I'd been with. Intention mattered. River said people had to want certain things in order for the tea to work, but he didn't see it the way I did because he didn't have Wela as a grandmother. She served it with the intention already made. I never wanted to forget that night all those years ago, but I did. I didn't want to forget anything in my life, but I had, and now I remembered all of it clearly. I remembered the screaming matches in my house. I remembered the anger and the pain caused. I remembered how volatile they'd been behind closed doors and how I smiled through all of it the following day because I was forced to forget it.

I sat through the rest of the Mass with my mother, because despite everything, she was my mother and I loved her. When she went to her sister's house with my grandmother, I kissed her goodbye, knowing it would be the last time I saw her. When I parked my Vespa in front of the house, I walked inside like a woman on a mission, packing bags of clothes and throwing them outside, far enough away from the house, before taking my own bag outside and setting it beside my Vespa.

I walked into the kitchen and threw everything inside the big tin trash bin on the kitchen floor before soaking it with gasoline and starting a fire inside it. I burned the leaves first, watching as they withered inside the bin, and then, I grabbed the container of gasoline and walked around the house, saying a prayer as I went.

By the time I reached the door and set the match, I'd made my peace with everything. I walked out and put on my helmet, grabbing my bag and reversing the Vespa to the street. I watched the flames for a moment, watched the black smoke as it took over. My grandmother would curse me for this. My mother would get over it and rebuild, but would probably be upset at me as well. I was fine with both of those things because despite that, I wasn't going to let the Caliban Manor go down alone. Not when the house that caused it all was still standing.

Not in my lifetime.

CHAPTER THIRTY-THREE

One year later

WHOEVER SAID TIME EASED PAIN WAS A LIAR. EVERY TIME I thought of River, my heart squeezed tighter than the last. I hadn't even dreamed of him since I left Pan. A part of me wanted to make a tea with the dried-up remnants of leaves I'd found in the pocket of my jacket when I unpacked my clothes, but I couldn't live with myself if I forgot him.

"It's beautiful here," Dee said, sighing as she sipped her drink.

"It is." I smiled, looking out into the water.

"What made you pick Santorini?" Martín asked. "Was it our wedding?"

"Of course, it was your wedding." I rolled my eyes, smiling as I shook my head. "Because I totally knew you were going to pick Santorini to elope in when I chose to move here."

Dee laughed. "Well, thank God for you. You've made this elopement possible by booking everything for us. Maybe you have a future as an elopement travel agent or something."

"After dealing with one bridezilla? No, thank you." I raised an eyebrow.

"You deserve a medal." Martín laughed. "The pictures have been nice. Who knew there were this many decaying houses on an island formed in two thousand BC?"

"Right?" Dee laughed. "The message boards have been going crazy with their talk about the Lost City of Atlantis."

"Have you found it yet?" Martín asked.

"I haven't looked." I laughed. "Besides, they've found a lot of proof that Atlantis is deep beneath Doñana for me to even go on that hunt."

I didn't even bring up the fact that the mere thought of searching for a lost city that was now undersea made me feel like crying. As it was, crying was the only thing I seemed to do when I was sitting in my therapist's office. I cried, I laughed, I cried some more. It was healthy to let it all out, she said. Still, all the therapy in the world couldn't cure the loneliness I felt.

"Have you met anyone?" Dee asked. "A male anyone."

"Not really." It wasn't a total lie. I had met a few guys here, but I wasn't interested.

"You will. Soon you'll meet a golden Greek god and he'll sweep you off your feet," Martín said.

I laughed and drained my drink. I wasn't ready to meet anyone. I didn't say that aloud because I didn't want to have to explain myself or lie to my friends.

"So, what else is on your itinerary while you're here?" I asked.

"Actually, we're going to try to find Atlantis," Dee said. "Which, now that you said that it's in Spain, I guess we won't."

"I don't think you'll find it during a snorkeling trip." I laughed. "But I'm sure it'll be just as magical as you envisioned."

"It will be. You should join us," Martín said.

"When?"

"In an hour actually." He glanced at his watch.

"Oh." I pouted. "I can't. I have a house to take a picture of. For the real estate company, not The Haunt."

"Bummer," Dee said. "But yay for making money."

"Yay for making money." I took some money out and Martín stopped me.

"It's on us."

"No way. You're here for your wedding and I know Greece is spectacular, but don't think you're fooling me for a second by saying you're not getting married here because of me." I shot them a look.

"We couldn't get married without you. We wouldn't have met if not for you," Dee said, raising an eyebrow. "By the way, Jose is also coming. He should be getting here later today."

"Oh, fun." I smiled wide and hoped I could keep it looking genuine.

I loved Jose, but I hadn't given him the tea I'd made Dee and Martín. Jose would remember everything that happened. He'd remember River Caliban. He'd remember watching the tsunami hit. His house had been flooded by its remnants, after all. I gave Dee and Martín a hug and kiss goodbye, promising them I'd see them at the ceremony tomorrow and walked up the cobblestoned street and looked at the address in my hand. To my surprise, the address wasn't too far away from Venetsanos\Winery, which was where I'd just had lunch with Martín and Dee. Still, I climbed on my Vespa and drove the rest of the way, blinking away the sand that hit my eyes as I drove. It was pretty secluded, as far as houses in Santorini went. I stopped in front of the gate and pushed the button to ring the bell.

"Hello?" It was a female voice.

"Hi, I'm Penelope Guzman. I'm here to take pictures of the property."

The gates opened in front of me before I even finished my sentence and I drove in slowly, stopping just past the gates and getting down to take pictures of the lot. There was a huge circle in the middle that looked like a helicopter landing pad. To the right, there was a covered area for cars, and way ahead, there was a blindingly white house. It was similar to most of the houses here, whitest of whites overlooking the bluest of blue water. A woman with long, dark brown hair stepped out of the house and waved at me. I hopped back on the Vespa and drove it to the carport, parking it beside a small white BMW.

"I'm sorry I'm late," I said, rushing to take the helmet off and hang it from the handle.

"It's no problem at all," she said, smiling as she shook my hand. "I'm Berenice."

"Penelope. As you know." I smiled back. "This place is beautiful. Secluded but beautiful."

"Very secluded. The owner owns the lots on either side of it as well, so they will probably remain empty." She glanced at me. "You won't have to include that in the listing though."

"Since they're not selling the lots you mean?"

"No, since the listing is only for vacation rentals."

"Oh." I nodded. "I didn't know that."

"Definitely include the helipad."

I laughed. "I did."

"Please, come on inside." She moved out of the way and let me start taking pictures, glancing at her watch.

"I am really so sorry I'm late," I said again, realizing I probably messed up her entire itinerary for the day. "My friends are getting married here and it's been hectic."

"It's really no problem," she assured me. "I may have to step out to take a phone call with my son's teacher, but aside from that, this is the only thing on my schedule today." She smiled. "It's my anniversary."

"Aw, that's nice." I moved on to the dining room and tried not to gasp at the view coming from the large windows at the end of the room. I glanced at her after snapping a few pictures. "I'm sorry. I'm not used to taking pictures of new houses. This is beautiful."

"Very luxurious, right?"

"Very."

"This is the master bedroom, you'll find a door that leads to the backyard there." She held up her phone, which was obviously ringing. "I'm sorry, but I need to step out to take this."

"It's not a big deal. I can show myself around." I smiled as I watched her go before going into the master bedroom, bathroom, closet, and finally, looking out into the yard.

Jesus.

I took a breath as I stepped outside. There was a pool, a large sitting area and an outdoor kitchen, and a long ledge that held another sitting area, which had been perfectly staged for pictures, with a small table and two chairs. I walked around, snapping photos, in awe of it before lowering my camera to take in the view in front of the ocean and other islands in front of me. I closed my eyes and inhaled, feeling the stillness for a moment.

"I've been waiting for you."

The voice came from behind me and made my eyes pop open. I turned around slowly, half anticipating this to be a dream, or a figment of my imagination. When I turned fully, I saw him, my heart hammering as I took him in. He was wearing brown loafers, blue chinos, and a white button-down shirt with the sleeves rolled up and the top couple of buttons undone. His hair was parted off to the side and his eyes were set on me as he blew out smoke from the cigarette in his hand. He flicked it away, taking one more step forward. I still couldn't move, could barely breathe.

"It's a bad habit. The smoking," he said. "Some people are allergic to it."

I nodded, the emotion in my throat too strong to let me speak. Finally, after the silence suspended for a moment too long, I swallowed and willed my heart to settle.

"How?" I whispered, not bothering to fight the tears that sprung in my eyes. "How?"

"How was I waiting for you?" He tilted his head, eyes scanning my face, amusement sparkling in his eyes. If I wasn't so stunned, I'd be mad. "You are here to take pictures, right?"

It struck me then, as I stood there, that maybe he didn't remember me. Maybe, maybe he'd survived the un-survivable because he'd taken the leaves and had forgotten me. Maybe, maybe he'd . . . I blinked and stopped trying to justify this to myself. Some things are inexplicable. Hadn't he once said that?

I swallowed and took a deep breath. He walked forward, his shoes tapping against the concrete as he closed the distance between us.

"You're so much more beautiful than I remembered, little witch." His eyes were still searching my face. I started crying then, really crying, burying my face in my hands to try to contain myself, and failing, because how do you contain such emotions?

"How?" I asked again, against my hands, wiping my tears in one swift, unattractive motion and meeting his gaze again.

"You wouldn't believe me if I told you."

"I'd believe anything you told me."

"Really?" He quirked an eyebrow. "It's a series of impossibilities."

I stared at him for a long moment before bringing a hand up to touch his face, to make sure this was real. I pinched myself then, again and again, and pinched his arm too, which made him laugh. I didn't find any of this funny.

"What are you?" I asked after a moment. "What are you, really?"

"Yours. If you'll have me."

I laughed through the tears, because of all of the things he could have said, that was the most perfect. "Anywhere? Any time?"

"Until the end of time." He grabbed the nape of my neck, pulled me to him, and kissed me.

CHAPTER THIRTY-FOUR

RIVER AND I WERE TANGLED IN WHITE SHEETS, LOOKING OUT into the sunset that bathed Santorini. You could see all of the ships, the islands, the deep blue water. It was a dream. I felt as though it was a dream. The thought made me panic, but I shook it away. This was real, and if it was a dream, I didn't want to wake up. I glanced up at River and found him watching me.

"You still haven't explained to me how you're here, alive and well."

"You didn't give me a chance." He grinned, kissing my forehead. His expression turned serious when he pulled back and brought a hand to my back, his fingers gliding over the few scars and welts that had already developed. "Tell me about this."

"Not yet." I swallowed, shaking my head.

"Mine are gone." He searched my eyes. "What the hell did you do, Penelope?"

"What did *you* do?" I sat up, bringing the sheet up with me in hopes to cover myself, but knowing it was futile.

"I wished for you to live."

"I wished the same for you." I glanced away, at the blue water.

"That's bullshit." He sat up as well, reaching for me and pinching my chin so I'd look at him. "What did you do?"

"Tell me what happened to you and where you've been this past year and I'll tell you what I did."

"The Manor collapsed. We were hit hard by a wave. My father died." River paused, swallowing before continuing. "One minute I was sitting underneath the tree with him and the next I was sitting on the Devil's Chair, sitting on the chair, but floating at sea. I swam to shore. I went to Dolly's, to my apartment—"

"That wasn't a dream."

"I don't know. I can't say what that was. All I know is that I couldn't stay." He shook his head. "My body was dragged away, dragged back to the chair, back across the iron gate. I was just out there, stranded, floating on top of a structure that shouldn't have floated at all."

He looked at me briefly. "I don't think I'd ever cried before, if I had I can't remember, but that night, as I vacillated between what once was Dolos Island and Pan Island, I cried. When I woke up again, I was in the Bahamas." He sighed.

"It took me months to get to the States, but during my time in the Bahamas, I went to see a witch that was also passing through. She told me I'd been freed. The curse had been lifted, and that made me panic because if I was free and alive, what did it mean for you? I went to Florida, to Amelia Island, but you weren't there. There was no sign of you there at all and I thought . . . I thought . . . " When he looked at me, his expression was pained. I set a hand on his and wiped my cheeks with the other. "What did you do, Penelope?"

"What I had to." I licked my lips, tasting the salt on them. "I burned my family's house. Burned the leaves. I told him that if he set you free, I'd endure his pain. I'd endure the suffering caused by the souls he'd taken in."

River shut his eyes, swallowing hard. "Why would you do that?"

"Because I love you too much to watch you suffer," I said loudly. "Because I didn't want to live in a world that you weren't a part of."

"Penelope," he whispered, opening his eyes. He brought a hand to my face, wiping my tears. "My world was over the moment you left that island."

"It wasn't. It didn't have to be." I wiped my face again, hating the pain in my chest. "It was the only way to undo the curse."

"I hate that he has any part of you. I hate that you did that for me."

"But I get to have you." I cupped his face.

"I know how this feels." He tapped a scar. "I know how much it hurts when you get new ones."

"You were ten when you started getting them. Ten years old, River. I'll survive it just fine."

He shook his head, glancing away briefly.

"How'd you find me?" I asked after a moment.

"The Haunt." He smiled at me. "You started posting pictures in Greece, and then more and more here in Santorini, and here I am."

"And now you're putting this beautiful house up for rent to vacationers," I said, smiling.

"Not really." His eyes crinkled as he looked at me. "It was just a ploy to get you here. I just bought it last week, but I didn't know what your plans were. I could stay here forever, but only if you're going to live in it with me."

"What?" My heart thumped harder.

He kissed my nose. "If it feels like home, we'll make it home."

"River Caliban." I sat up straighter, letting the sheet fall from my hand so that I could grab both sides of his face. "The only thing that feels like home to me is you."

"Good, because the feeling's mutual." He pressed his lips against me then and kissed me with the fire of a thousand souls trying to get back to their other half.

EPILOGUE

"**W**HEN WE SAID YOU'D FIND A GREEK GOD IN NO TIME, WE were not expecting you to actually go out and find one," Dee said, eyes wide on River.

"I hope it's okay that I brought him," I whispered. "It was all so very last minute."

"Um, yeah, as if we'd ever turn away a super-hot guy from our wedding guest list."

I laughed, then looked over at Jose, who was uncharacteristically quiet. Dee squeezed my hands and went to change. Jose stood quickly and rushed over to me.

"What the fucking fuck?" he whisper-shouted. "He's supposed to be dead. How does Dee not remember this?"

I bit my lip. "If I told you, you wouldn't believe me."

"Try me." He raised an eyebrow. "I am from the fable capital of the world, after all."

"I gave Dee and Martín tea leaves and set the intention that they'd forget," I said, rushing to explain myself. "It was too much for me, I can't even imagine how traumatizing it would be for you guys. I'm sorry I couldn't make you forget."

"I'm glad you didn't. How else was I supposed to fight my insurance company into covering what the flood damaged if I had no memory of it?" Jose shook his head. "So, they didn't die?"

"They did." I looked down, hating that lives were lost at all. "He survived."

"I can't imagine how," Jose said. "I saw the tsunami from my window. I can't . . . it was un-survivable."

"Yet here we are." I looked at him again.

"And Dolos will just become another fable, like Atlantis, like Port Royal would be, had it not been for all of the witness accounts."

"People loves fables."

"And other lies." Jose's lips twisted. He thought about that for a long moment. When he looked at me again, he smiled. "I'm glad he's alive. I'm glad he's with you again."

"Thank you. So am I." I smiled back.

When we stepped into the church with Dee, Jose walked her down the aisle and I stood beside her at the altar. As the priest held Mass, River and I didn't take our eyes off each other. I felt something deep inside my ribs as they said their vows and smiled knowing that we had our own happily ever after ahead of us.

ClaireContrerasbooks.com

Twitter: @ClariCon

Insta: ClaireContreras

Facebook: www.facebook.com/groups/
ClaireContrerasBooks

OTHER BOOKS

The Trouble With Love
Fake Love
The Consequence of Falling
Because You're Mine
Half Truths
Twisted Circles
The Sinful King
The Naughty Princess

SECOND CHANCE DUET
Then There Was You
My Way Back to You

The Wilde One
The Player

THE HEART SERIES
Kaleidoscope Hearts
Torn Hearts
Paper Hearts
Elastic Hearts

DARKNESS SERIES
There is No Light in Darkness
Darkness Before Dawn

Made in the USA
Coppell, TX
01 June 2021

56693183R00152